Dalrymple J. Belgrave

Jack Warleigh - A Tale of the Turf and the Law

Vol. I

Dalrymple J. Belgrave

Jack Warleigh - A Tale of the Turf and the Law
Vol. I

ISBN/EAN: 9783337082567

Printed in Europe, USA, Canada, Australia, Japan

Cover: Foto ©Andreas Hilbeck / pixelio.de

More available books at **www.hansebooks.com**

BY

DALRYMPLE J. BELGRAVE

IN TWO VOLUMES

VOL. I.

LONDON—CHAPMAN AND HALL

LIMITED

1891

CONTENTS.

CHAPTER XIII.

JACK WARLEIGH.

CHAPTER I.

AN OLD GRAMMAR SCHOOL.

Saint Paul's Square, Fetchester, is full of easy-going prosperity : not of the bustling, restless kind one finds in a manufacturing town, but something that seems more solid, and suggests the three per cents : small profits and good security. There is a sense of rest about the place, and in the summer time, plenty of grateful shade.   On one side of the Square is St. Paul's church, with its church-yard, where the past generations of Fetchester folk peacefully sleep, under the deep shadows cast by elm trees.   The inscriptions on the grave stones show the same names, with the same callings, occurring again and again.   Sons have followed fathers as parsons, doctors, lawyers, butchers, mercers and so on : and centuries seem to have left but few scars on that quiet little midland town. Every three hours the bells in St. Paul's steeple chime out a plaintive old hymn tune, and listening to their cadence, one notes a rare harmony of scene and sound. Across the far end of the Square, runs the trim little High Street, and facing the church, there is a row of substantial red-brick houses, that have an air of home and easy quiet lives about them. The other side of the Square is formed by the buildings of the old Grammar School. There is little or no architectural beauty in the block, but its age lends a soothing sense of rest, and adds a charm to the surroundings. In front of the school stands a statue, "In ever grateful memory" of Sir William Wardour, its pious founder. The Grammar School boys were perhaps not "ever" duly grateful; sometimes when smarting from the effects of going up to the Reverend Arthur Paradine, with Arnold's Prose Exercises, they gazed at the pious Knight's presentment and wished that he had never lived, or at least found something better to do with his money.

On quiet summer days when the school

windows were open, a visitor standing in the Square might often have heard Mr. Paradine storming at his class. "Ha! Simpkins junior, so you don't know what the nominative is to the verb. In another fortnight, a young gentleman from Oxford will come down to examine you, and you won't be able to answer his questions, and he will say to me 'Mr. Paradine, I think it would be better to be more careful about the parsing, *about the parsing*,'" and the voice would repeat the words, again and again, as though it were some savage war-cry. Then would arise the sound of wailing and the cane.

A lady dressed in black would sometimes stand in the Square, within the shadow cast by the church, and nervously listen for that rich voice. She knew that Mr. Paradine was, in the main, a kindly gentleman, and that the boys,—with honest instinct, which makes them bear so little resentment for corporal punishment—liked him better than the other milder masters. For all that, her face would flush with anger, and she would long to make her way into the school, and give that ripe old scholar a bit of her mind. And she would have done so, too, only she dreaded the indignation which such a breach of school etiquette, on her

part, would have been received by her
boy.

Sometimes another figure, then very
familiar in the Fetchester Street, would
cross the Square with an accustomed half
swagger, half limp. It was the figure of
an elderly man, with a large curled and
dyed moustache, a white hat worn
jauntily on one side, who leaned somewhat
heavily on his stick, and he would smile
when he heard the sound, which held the
widow spell-bound : and as he put out a
gouty old hand, he would ask her if she
were not trembling lest her boy were
catching it from old Paradine. " Well,
if he is his father's son, he will know
how to take his punishment, Jack could,"
he would say, and then he would have
much to tell her of his old comrade Jack
Warleigh.

She never cared for these reminiscences
of her dead husband. It was pleasant
enough to her to hear him praised, and
old Major Chaffinch evidently thought
that his stories of wild nights at mess,
and of losses at play, and on the race-
course redounded much to his credit.
But the Jack Warleigh whose memory
the widow worshipped, and whom she
had only known a few months before
they were married, and then for a few

weeks after he was ordered off to the Crimea, to have his brave life squandered away at Balaklava, was a very different man from old Chaffinch's hero.

When the Major had finished his stories of the old days, he would usually ask after his friend Sir George Warleigh.

"A fine type of the good old school that, as hard as iron, by gad!" the Major would say.

Mrs Warleigh used not to find her father-in-law a pleasant subject of conversation. Before they were married, old Sir George had quarrelled bitterly with her husband, and he had made that quarrel an excuse for doing very little for her or her boy, when they were left rather badly off, after her husband's death.

She was the daughter of a Fetchester clergyman; she had gone back to live at her native town, and in due time had sent her boy Jack to be educated at the Grammar School.

Old Major Chaffinch would wind up his conversation by growling out a hope that his boys were getting their fair share of Mr. Paradine's attention—after which paternal wish, he would hobble off to the billiard-room at the "Swan," where he would sit and watch the game and give

the youth of Fetchester the benefit of his matured views of men and women.

Behind the Grammar School there was a red-brick house, with a pleasant shaded garden, that reached down to the river, which flows sluggishly through the old town. Sometimes there would cross the Square, to that house, on her way home from school, a girl of sixteen, a little girl, with features rather long for her face, a mass of golden brown hair hanging over her shoulders, and a pair of big eyes. A girl of whom one might foretell that she would grow into a very beautiful woman. She was Nelly Paradine, the daughter of the grim old second master at the Grammar School.

Perhaps, next to her boy, there was no one whom the widow loved more, and her soft face would light up as she talked with Nelly Paradine about her school and home life. Then they would hear a noise in the school buildings, of many boys rushing downstairs, and soon a jostling crowd of eager lads would surge out through the iron gates up the play-ground into the Square, and Jack Warleigh would run up to them, and half blushing, would shake hands with Nelly Paradine, and walk home with his mother, talking to her about his school.

As a rule, boys are somewhat shame-faced about being seen with their mothers and sisters in the streets, but no one thought of laughing at Jack Warleigh. He was the most popular boy in the school, though he was not by any means the most brilliant. At games he did fairly well. At his lessons he showed some talent, though not much application, but he took such punishment as came in his way, with a philosophic calm which in a way gained him the respect of the boys, and perhaps —of the master.

On Sunday afternoons there used to be a school service in the chancel at St. Paul's, which in those days was shut off from the rest of the church, in a manner which must have given rise to great scandal to such of the parishioners as were abreast of the age in questions of church restoration and ritual. There was a pew reserved for masters' families, and Nelly used to sit in this pew. Jack Warleigh, looking back to those days has a distinct memory of Nelly's face, as she sat there, under a painted glass window. He can hardly remember when it was that he first thought himself in love with her. Mrs. Warleigh used to watch the two together, when Nelly came to her house, as she often did, and, mother-like, she would indulge in a dream of the future.

Jack's life, unlike his father's, was to be a peaceful one. Old Sir George, on one of the few occasions on which he had shown any interest in his grandson, had promised to give him a family living. There was no one else in the family to take it, for his eldest son had died, leaving only one boy, George, while his youngest son, Cecil —the baronet had married a second time, late in life—who was his favourite, was not to be made a parson. Jack was too easy-going to trouble himself about the future. He certainly had no particular wish to be a clergyman, but he looked forward to Cambridge, as most schoolboys would, and the time that was to follow the delightful years to be spent at college seemed so far off that it was of no use troubling himself about it. Then he would be a different being altogether, so he thought.

Looked backed to, those days at Fetchester seemed to be altogether happy. Probably at the time, he had troubles enough as boys will: but from a distance he remembers best the easy flowing river, and the long half-holidays spent upon it, the boy companions who had not yet learnt the bad lessons the world teaches, and Nelly Paradine's honest brown eyes and golden hair, lit up by the sunlight that streamed through the painted glass window of St. Paul's church. Unlike boys who have gone away from home to school, there was no break in his early life. It was all Fetchester, and the story of his life meanders back until it is drowned in the sweet chimes from the old church tower. The quiet of St. Paul's Square was seldom broken.

Twice a year there were Assizes in the old Court House. They seldom lasted more than a day or two, and there seemed to be very little excuse for all the pomp and paraphernalia of judges, sheriff and javelin men; while the gentlemen of the bar grumbled bitterly at the pitiful lack of enterprise which could only produce a few wretched prisoners, most of whom artlessly pleaded guilty, and perhaps some one poor civil action. Once the place was startled by a cavalry regiment, on the line of march, coming into the town and taking up its quarters there for the night. Such an event had never happened—so it was said—since Prince Rupert's troopers filled the place, on the eve of a disastrous fight during the Great Rebellion.

That was a day which Jack Warleigh

will always remember, for after the parade had been dismissed, and the men had gone to their different billets, a young officer with a pleasant handsome face, and singularly winning manner, came up to a group of school-boys, of which he was one, and asked them if they belonged to the school, and if a boy of the name of Warleigh was there.

" How are you, young man ? " he said, when Jack came forward.

" I am your uncle, your half uncle— Cecil Warleigh, I remembered you were here, and thought I would give you a look up. I remember the governor talking about you, saying they were going to make a parson of you ; and you were to have Warleigh Rectory some day. I thought I'd take you to the pastry-cook—that was the sort of thing I used to like, when I was in the lower school at Eton, but you're past that." Jack Warleigh was seventeen, and stood over six feet high.

" Tell you what, you had better dine with us at mess, at the Swan.   It will be a scratch affair I daresay, but we'll do what we can for you."   Jack looked delighted at the notion of dining with the gallant Loyal Lancers, and was also very much taken with his kinsman.

" Shall I go and see the head-master

and ask leave for you? Ah! I forgot, you are a day-boy and live here with your mother. Well, you must tell her you are going to dine with me."

Jack pointed to a group of ladies, who were walking from the Square, and said his mother was there. She had come to see the Lancers.

"Ah, to be sure—why of course she would come to see us, your father was in the regiment—killed at Balaclava. I've often heard the Colonel talk of him," said Cecil. "I must go and speak with her."

The young officer made a good impression on Mrs. Warleigh, who felt the charm of his pleasant and good-natured manner. It had been rather a trying morning for her. The scene she had witnessed could not but remind her of the morning she had last seen the regiment, and taken her farewell of her husband ere he embarked for the Crimea.

"The Colonel and several of the older men in the regiment, will like to meet him," Cecil said, as he talked of Jack's dining with them: and the widow felt that it was right her son should go, though she was conscious of something like dread, at the thought of Jack having almost grown up and having so soon to face the temptations and dangers of manhood.

Jack never forgot that evening. He had never met any society so brilliant. The stories, the military chaff, the sparkle and dash of the whole thing, made a lasting impression upon him. There seemed to be no one at the mess who was so bright and popular as Cecil Warleigh.

After that dinner, Jack for some time thought of following in his father's footsteps, by becoming a soldier. But the thought of Cambridge, and a wish to please his mother, reconciled him to the notion of the Church. Nelly's influence also came in. When he was only nineteen there was a boy and girl engagement between them, and when he thought of his future life as a clergyman it always seemed that it would be shared with her.

For years Jack saw little of the relations whose name he bore. His grandfather had died, and his cousin, Sir George, who succeeded, had married soon after he left Cambridge, and had settled at Warleigh, and seemed to have forgotten his very existence.

CHAPTER II.

NELLY PARADINE.

WHEN Jack went up to Cambridge, though he did not show any very great devotion to his studies he became rather a distinguished undergraduate. He rowed stroke of his college boat, and would—so it was said—get into the University eight, if he only stuck to it and was not drawn away by other distractions. Besides rowing, he played cricket, occasionally rode, usually found his way to Newmarket when there was any racing on. He became very popular with almost every set in college, except the reading set. When he went back to Fetchester in the vacation, the boys at the school regarded him with awe and admiration, though some people shook their heads at sundry stories of wild supper parties and rowdy escapades which he was said to have taken part in. Among those who were not altogether pleased with what they heard was Nelly

Paradine. Joe Paradine, her younger brother, was a fellow of a small college at Cambridge, and he brought home with him a plentiful supply of stories which were not to Jack Warleigh's credit. "He never read, he lived in the fastest set in the college, he was up to his eyes in debt, and was certain to ruin his mother and go to the dogs. If he ever took his degree and went into the Church it would be a scandal and a disgrace to the Establishment." It was surprising that the fellow of "Cats," should have known so much about the doings of the undergraduates of St. George. But Joe Paradine the plodder had always cherished a grudge against Jack Warleigh, for years before when he was a big boy at the school, and Jack but a little chap, Jack had kicked Joe's shins and set his authority at defiance. Joe had very little of interest to relate to any one. A strict devotion to mathematics, which had helped him to gain his college successes, does not as a rule, make a man shine in society. So he found Jack's misdoings a serviceable topic of conversation.

"The youngster is quite right to have his fling before they make a parson of him. He is a chip of the old block, there is plenty of the wild Warleigh blood in him, by George!" old Chaffinch would often declare with glee. Whenever he heard any wild tale of Jack's goings on, he would trumpet it abroad, thinking it told much to the credit of his old comrade's son. Nelly looked very grave when she heard of these stories. She had only too good reason to know how a University Rake's progress ended. Sam Paradine, her eldest brother, had been the brilliant boy of his family. He acquired all his father's scholarship, and he had far more genius. Old Paradine took care not to favour him, but when Sam was quite young, and at the top of his class, boys had noticed the grim face of the schoolmaster relax, and a smile come over it as he listened to his son do his work. He was always first at school, and he took the School Exhibition and another good scholarship at Oxford, then he went up to the University with a career before him which every one prophesied would be splendid; and it was splendid—in a way. After his second term, it is doubtful whether Sam ever found time to open a book. He was in what is called the very best set at Christ Church, and was the most popular man of his day. Young men of rank, and rich young men who wished to be in fashion, and all sorts and conditions of undergraduates, tried to know Sam Paradine, and repeated his sayings—which to speak truth were commonplace enough—and made much of him. And Sam accepted the situation. It was necessary that such a popular man as he was, should spend money. He spent such money as he could get hold of, and did wonders in the way of running into debt. His income with his Exhibition scholarship and the small allowance which his father could afford him, amounted to about two hundred and fifty pounds a year. At one time he kept two horses : his dinners were the best in the college, his orders to the new cigar and wine merchant, who started at Oxford in his time, were the most princely which that enterprising tradesman ever received. Almost all the Oxford tradesmen had his name in their books, and at the same time he dealt with those of the metropolis. Even the London hotel-keepers were induced to let him have a running account, and he ran up heavy bills at two famous hostelries, where he would stay in the vacations, and entertain with the splendour of an American millionaire. In his second year the crash came. It was splendid and complete. He was sent away from college, and though he was made a bankrupt, there were some debts, which, for reasons best known to Mr. Paradine, Sam, and the money lender to whom they were owed, had to be paid. That date marked an era in the family history, after which there had to be much pinching, screwing, and discomfort. The furniture got shabbier, and was not renewed. There was less money forthcoming for household expenses. Mr. Paradine's stock of old port wine came to an end, and the cellar was not replenished : but gin and water, and plenty of it too, took its place. A drawn, haggard look, for the first time came into the old man's rubicund countenance.

Nelly saw very little of Sam, after that date. He went up to London, and for a year or so some of his old splendour hung round him. After a while he began to show a greasy and shabby appearance, his face became bloated, and he was believed to be getting a living, somehow or the other, on the fringe of literature. Little was known of him at Fetchester, his name never being mentioned in his old home. Some girls might see something romantic in a wild reckless college career, but Nelly was not one of them. She thought of her brother Sam, and dreaded lest Jack Warleigh should be following in his footsteps. So she shook her head and took a serious view of Jack's delinquencies. About this time there had been a change in Fetchester, which had a great deal of influence upon Nelly, as also upon other of the townspeople. The good old vicar of St. Paul's had died, and been succeeded by a priest who for some time kept the little town in a ferment, and made his name and his church very familiar in the ecclesiastical courts.

The Reverend Henry Latimer, or "Father Latimer" as he preferred to be styled, made things lively at Fetchester, and woke up a spirit of militant protestantism. Mr. Bloggs, the butcher in the High Street, found himself impelled to protest in church, against the *merry-andrewing and antics*, as he called it of the parson ; and afterwards had to go to prison instead of paying the fine, which the magistrates were obliged to impose upon him for brawling. Major Chaffinch, whose attendance at church, had been— to put it mildly—irregular, came to the front as a protestant champion. Going to church became quite interesting, for there was no telling what the parson would be up to next, and his doings on the Sunday would be the subject for much talk during the week. The Vicar,

of course, had his party. It consisted
of a large proportion of the women-folk,
some womanly men of the better classes,
and a good many poor people, to whom, to
do him justice, he was extremely chari-
table. Nelly was of the vicar's party.
Perhaps if Fetchester had not been so
dull, she would not have been so devoted
an adherent. As it was, she worked
vestments, joined a guild of young ladies,
who swept out the church, and did the
work which in more benighted times en-
abled an old and deserving woman to
earn a livelihood. She also attended
countless services, and even went so far
as to attend confessional, when the vicar
introduced the rite. People wondered
that her father did not put a stop to it ; but
he only said " she was too sensible a girl
not to get wiser in time." Mr. Paradine
himself took things easily, and in church
slept through the vicar's addresses, which
were directed against the principles of
the Reformation, as he had slept through
the late vicar's prosy orthodoxy.

Jack Warleigh, when he came home
from Cambridge, chaffed Nelly about her
church sweeping and ritualism, and did
not guess how much his chaff displeased
her. Some of Jack's remarks came to
the ears of the vicar, who had a feminine

propensity for listening to petty gossip and interfering in the private affairs of his parishioners. He heard some talk of an engagement between Jack and Nelly, and being one of those who "rush in where angels fear to tread," thought that to talk to a young girl of her lover was a duty for which he was quite suited. So he found an opportunity of saying a word to Nelly about Jack. First he warned her against Mrs. Warleigh. The widow like a good woman had accepted all her religion from her father, an excellent divine, whose views were moderately low-church, and she expressed her horror at the new doings. The priest showed Nelly how Mrs. Warleigh's disobedience to the Church bore fruit in her son. That abandoned young man, who was not only hopelessly vicious, but scoffed at the Church and her priests, was on the side of her ignorant and contemptible oppressors, and intended for the sake of earthly profit to take Holy Orders. He had heard that Nelly hesitated to repudiate an engagement she had entered into with this repro-bate. For his sake, even if he were not utterly lost, she ought to overcome any sinful love she might have for him. Nelly's womanly instinct told her that no man had a right to talk to her about Jack in this way, but her church feeling conquered, and she listened to him, and then doubted if she ought not to obey him.

Their conversation had begun in the vestry of St. Paul's, and was continued in the churchyard. And it happened that the subject of it—Jack Warleigh—was waiting for Nelly, lounging by the railing of the Grammar School, talking to old Chaffinch.

"Jack, my boy," said the latter, as he stared at the vicar with a malignant eye, "they tell me that you're sweet in that quarter, if you are, look after that fox of a vicar. I know the breed—dash 'em. He has as big a bag of tricks as any monkey. Hang me! if he hasn't set up confessing. Dashed if I wouldn't—" but the rest of the major's speech was utterly unsuited for reproduction: so rich was it in illustration and invective. When Nelly met Jack she felt half ashamed of herself, something told her that it would be better for her not to let the parson come between them. But the latter's bad luck prompted him to speak upon just the wrong subject.

"Well, Nellie, have you been confessing your sins, or has it been a meeting of the holy dusters?"

"You know you ought not to talk in

that way about sacred subjects," Nelly said, more angry than she would have been if she had not felt doubtful as to whether or no she ought to have let the vicar speak to her as he had done.

"What nonsense, Nelly! What can there be sacred in a lot of you girls taking it into your heads to do old Mrs. Grimes' work, and sweep out the church?" answered Jack, still in blissful ignorance of the coming storm.

"It is not nonsense, Mr. Warleigh. We think differently, so differently that it is impossible for us to be friends, and for me to respect or care for you. No, I am in earnest, I intended to say this as soon as I saw you. What we spoke of once, must be all over. We have both altered. If you had cared for me, your life would have been different and you would have been steadier, and not have learned to sneer at everything that is good. You, who think of becoming a clergyman."

"I don't say that I am as good as I should be," pleaded Jack, "I have been wild and idle perhaps, but when I become a parson, I intend to do my duty. You know what made me determine to take the living. Nelly! you and I are not going to quarrel about this ritualistic rot."

"We must each go our own way. If

you choose to commit the sin of taking orders for an unworthy motive, I'll have nothing to do with it," answered Nelly, looking very white and determined.

In the distance, turning the corner of the Square, Jack saw the long shambling figure of the vicar. He remembered old Chaffinch's words, and he lost his temper.

" You have allowed that man-milliner to talk to you about me, and permitted him to interfere between us. You seem to think because he calls himself a priest he may say what he likes to you," angrily blurted out Jack.

" Stop. You need not say any more. I will never speak to you again. You have insulted me," said Nelly, and she turned round and walked away. Jack stood staring at her, hardly realizing at first how serious the breach between them was.

So it ended ; for from that day they were no longer even friends. Mrs. Warleigh thought Nelly had proved herself to be heartless. What mother is just to the girl whom she thinks has made her son unhappy? She thought it Nelly's fault that Jack was wild and reckless ; and the friendship between Nelly and the widow, which had been very sweet to both of them, seemed to be broken and at an end.

CHAPTER III.

A MORNING'S REFLECTIONS.

JACK WARLEIGH'S sufferings were perhaps a good deal less acute than his mother believed them to be. He was hurt and angry, and considered that Nelly had treated him badly.

He felt that if he had chosen to give way to dissipation he would have an excuse for it, and on going up for the next term, he went his own way and got into "rows" with the Dons—ran up numerous ticks with the tradesmen of Cambridge, and generally behaved himself as if the morrow with its reckonings would never come.

One morning, however, it dawned upon him that it had come. His first sensation had been a bad headache. Then he experienced a dull sense of impending trouble. He knew that something was wrong, though his drowsy senses did not, at first, tell him what it was, and gradually, one after another, what seemed to be either the incidents of the evening before, or the conclusion of some horrible dream, came out uncertainly to his misty senses. Was it a dream? Jack Warleigh asked himself. So far, there was no corroboration except the head-ache. Certainly all he remembered was wild and confused enough for a night-mare. Incident seemed to have followed incident, with a rapidity that was hardly real. But then there was the headache, and there on a chair by his bedside was a slip of white paper, on which there was a curt notice, half lithographed : 'Mr. Warleigh to call on Mr. Perker at 10.30.' With a sickening sense that he was going to see more that would distress him, he crawled to the door that led into his sitting-room. On a table there was a clean white cloth and his breakfast laid out in orderly fashion. But that only emphasized its surroundings. Huddled in a heap in a corner of the room was a confused mass of legs of chairs, the back of a sofa, fragments of a sideboard, and other bits of what was once the furniture of his college rooms; the door was smashed in and the windows broken.

"Well, I shan't want 'em, that's one thing, my occupancy of these or any other rooms in Cambridge is at an end. I remember that enough happened last night, to get me 'sent down' twenty times over," Jack said to himself, with a sigh.

"Ain't it hawful, sir? Lor! when I come into these rooms this morning, sir, I was took that aback that I goes into the pantry, an' sets down on the floor and 'as a good cry. That's what I did, sir. The furnitur' that I hev' a dusted and took care of like as if it was my hown. And the sight o' empty bottles," said a husky voice, and a little old woman with a dirty face, red eyes, and a certain unsteadiness of gait and manner—which suggested that she had sought consolation from some of the not quite empty bottles—came into the sitting-room from the pantry.

"Ah, this finishes me, Mrs. Gruppy, 'it's all up with the army,' as Balbus said."

"And well he might say so, sir : though if he was here last night, I dare say he was as bad as enny of 'em—that it should come to this! To think of your dear Mar, what she'd say. When I thinks of 'er sittin' on one o' them theer cheers at that 'ere table, when she come hup in the May term—eatin' luncheon—little did I ever think it 'ud come to this, for I'm a mother myself and 'as a feelin' 'art."

" Confound you, get out of this and don't stand jabbering there," shouted Jack Warleigh : for the old woman's maunderings had touched him on rather a sore point.

Mrs. Gruppy took herself off, declaiming as to her feelings when she came into the rooms in the morning—" Though the porter at the gate told her that there had been goings on at Mr. Warleigh's the night before, she wouldn't have believed that the rooms were in the state they were. " Not if he'd gone down on his bended knees, and swored it on the Bible."

" Yes, I ought to have thought about that before," Warleigh groaned, as he followed up the train of reflections which the old woman's words had suggested. " Ah, what an infernal fool he had made of himself ! "

The yesterday had been most disastrous, and yet it had begun so well.

At ten o'clock he had left his rooms on his way to Long Jones, his tutor's. Newmarket races were going on, but though the day before had been the Cambridgeshire, and plenty of men had pressed him to go with them, he had resisted all temptations, and stayed at home and read.

But just as he neared the tutor's door, a passing wagonette pulled up, and a chorus of cheery voices shouted out his name.

"Jack Warleigh! Jump in and come with us to Newmarket," shouted the driver, one Jack Raggles of Magdalene.

"Can't, I'm off to Long Jones' to coach," said Jack.

"Long Jones! what rot," said Raggles. "Come on, I've a real good thing for the two-year-old race to-day—*a certainty*—my tout has written to me about it. He is a wonderful clever chap is my tout. I gave him a pair of race-glasses the other day, and he tells me he has seen a trial with 'em already. Jump in, we'll come back with a hatful of money," said Mr. Raggles, who had the reputation of being a very deep fellow indeed.

The day before Jack had beaten the tempter on a good square fair fight. He had kept away from Newmarket in the Cambridgeshire day. But now he was knocked out of time by a chance blow. There was really no reason why he should have gone. Raggles was just the sort of man his good sense told him it would be well to fight shy of, nevertheless Jack Warleigh jumped into the wagonette, and in less time than it takes to tell, was bowling along in the direction of the famous heath.

Jack had been much impressed with Mr. Raggles' tout when that gentleman sidled up to them after the first race. He was a red-faced man with a chronic droop of the left eyelid and an air of much mystery.

" You'd have to back ' Beggarman ' for the two-year-old race, Squire," he said whispering in Mr. Raggles' ear, and making the whole wagonette smell of spirits. " Go ' nap ' on it ! "

" But you told me ' Early Mo,' " said Raggles, almost piteously, for he felt a sickening dawn of doubt.

The red-nosed man shook his head with an air of intense knowingness. In his mind he was reflecting on the danger of drink when he had to remember *which* certainty he had given to each of his patrons.

" It's a certainty for ' Early Mo,' bar ' Beggarman,' back 'em both, there ain't no one can tell straighter than that, there ain't nothing else in the race goin'."

" But one won't stand to win much, backing the two favourites," said Raggles piteously.

" That's just the thing, young gents ; you're 'ankerin' arter winners at thirty-three to one. I might say one of the hothers and chance it, but I says what I knows, an' when I can't pick between two, I owns it honest and says, *back 'em both*," and Mr. Bulbeck reflected that he had got rather well out of his stupid mistake. Then mysteriously saying that he was going to have a word with a party in the paddock " as will tell me somethink, Squire, as I shall 'ave to tell you," he slipped away. They would have been surprised perhaps to have seen him sidle up to another young gentleman, and, tapping him on the shoulder, inform him that the two-year-old race was a moral for Monopole, and so on going from client to client giving them various information, until he had given every horse in the race. So that he watched the race which was won by neither Early Mo nor Beggarman— with the pleasing consciousness that he had done a good turn to some one. But though his information was so faulty, his manner was as impressive as ever, when he came back to Mr. Raggles and his friends, who were all losers.

" Hevery-think haltered in the weighing room and the money all shifted at the last minute : dear, dear, there'll be warnin's hoff and the dooce to pay about this 'ere, an' serves 'em right, I says," was his apology, and not one whit abashed he whispered a " good thing " for the next race, which somehow they all believed in.

There was something beautiful in the child-like faith with which they clung to

Mr. Bulbeck. Without him Mr. Raggles felt that he would cease to be the knowing character he had always been, and would have no rock to cling to. The others followed Raggles, for they had always believed in his judgment, and the consequence was Jack Warleigh returned to Cambridge, having lost more money than he could afford.

If when they got back to Cambridge they had separated, it would not have been so bad. But young men who have got into mischief find it difficult to separate. They dined at the Hoop together. After dinner they went out for a stroll. Their evil genius led them to the market square, where it happened that a disturbance made by some undergraduates at an entertainment at the Town Hall, had led to a mild town and gown row. Raggles was in the thick of it at once, attempting to rescue a man who had been arrested by the police. Perhaps it was lucky for them that the Proctor came up, and taking their names and colleges, sent them home. By that time they were endeared to each other by a sense of troubles undergone together. They determined to spend the rest of the evening at Jack Warleigh's rooms. On the way they met a very mild freshman, whom one of them knew. It would be capital fun to ask him too, some one said. They finished the evening with a vengeance. They had songs, then there was a general bear-fighting, in which a good deal of furniture was smashed, then more songs with chorus. Some of these choruses were of the stupid, objectionable, old-fashioned Cambridge type. While one of them was being howled out, some one at the window, which looked into the street, discovered that the Proctor and his bulldogs, as the Proctor's men are called, were standing outside listening. Probably he was pondering over the non-survival of the fittest in melody, and declaring he would even sooner have made a good many of our laws, than the particular song he was listening to.

"Throw something at him," said Raggles of Magdalene.

"What a lark!" said another of the party, the freshman who had been asked by chance, and who hitherto had done nothing to add to the harmony of the evening. "I'll have a shot," and taking up a bag of eggs which, had been brought in by Jack's bed-maker that day, he threw one of them at the Proctor, and by sheer bad luck—for he was in no condition to aim straight—hit him between the eyes.

"You young idiot!" said Jack, and for a minute, dismay fell upon the party. But Raggles was "going down" at the end of the term, and cared not a straw whether he was sent down or went down on his own account.

"Let's stand a siege," he shouted, "we shall soon have the dons on to us, don't let 'em in. You're game, Warleigh, ain't you?"

"Yes, I'm game," said Jack. "One may as well die game."

Soon there was a knock at the sported oak, and one of the fellows of the college was heard demanding to be let in. He was answered by derisive shouts and yells.

"Ah! he's gone to get the porter to open the oak; let's barricade the inside door," said Raggles, and they began to move furniture, upset the sideboard, and did more of the breaking.

Jack no longer cared a bit. After all he could only be expelled. He was perfectly reckless and mad with excitement. The outside door was opened, and this was answered by a yell of defiance from the besieged. They could identify the leader of the storming party as the junior dean, who had made himself unpopular. Some of the men who knew him shouted out his name, coupled with personal remarks calculated to hurt his feelings. Mr. Raggles, who did not know him, contented himself with shouting at him by name, calling him vituperative epithets which would suit any one.

"I say, why should not we bolt out of here? These bars ain't over strong," suggested one of the party who had opened the window.

"Right you are, my boy, that would sell 'em," said Raggles. "But what does Jack say?"

"Capital idea; make haste about it," said Jack.

It was a match which would hold out longest, the door or the window bar? The latter went first. The besieged party, one by one, squeezed through and dropped into the dark lane outside. The valiant Raggles alone remained.

"I'll see you through it, old chap," said he. "There goes the door. Produce the classics!" And then, after pausing a moment to collect his dignity, the dean entered.

Jack was standing at the table with a Juvenal and a Greek Lexicon before him. Raggles, with great difficulty, was balancing himself on a one-legged chair, the only one that remained, and was hard at work at an algebra and a Latin dictionary.

"Curious conduct of a clergyman!" said Raggles, as he eyed the junior dean reproachfully. "Can't a man read in this college without being drawn by the the dons? Most officious I must say." "Hulloa!" and he broke off as the wreck he was sitting on finally collapsed, and he sat down heavily on a broken bottle.

Jack remembered that his friend was soon afterwards persuaded by the porters to take his departure, saying, as he picked up some of Jack's books, that he would go and read in Magdalene, where he could have quiet, and the dons left him alone. Of the dean's leave-taking Jack had not quite such a clear idea, but he remembered that it was not pleasant or cordial.

They would have him up before the Master and senior fellows, Jack thought, as he finished his toilet, and he would have an opportunity, for the first time, of making the acquaintance of that distinguished scholar, the head of his college. He had never spoken to him before, and he didn't suppose he ever should again. He put his hand into his pocket, and pulling out the note-book he was taking with him to his coach the morning before, he threw it at the heap of broken furniture. He wouldn't want that any more. He had finished with Greek and

Latin Accidence, and Paley's Evidences. Then he gloomily pondered over the idea suggested by the old woman's babbling. Yes, it would be a bad day when he went home, expelled and disgraced. He ought to have thought of that before, however, but, hang it! he seemed to have thought of nothing at all the day before.

"Come in, it's not locked," he cried, as he heard a knock at the splintered door.

A young man with a pale face, in which remorse and biliousness were the prevailing characteristics, came in ; and gazed round at the smashed furniture :—

" Warleigh, this is terrible : what will they do to us do you think ? " he said, all but bursting into tears.

" You're not the man you were last night, my boy. There was no holding you then," said Jack, as he contemplated his visitor's face and thought what a fool he had been to let such a young ass get him into so much trouble.

" Oh, my father will be so awfully cut up if I am ' sent down.' He thinks such a lot of Cambridge and degrees and all that sort of thing. It was a precious pull for him sending me up here."

And the youngster did actually begin to cry.

Jack looked at him, and felt that he could follow his example. His mother had not too much money, and the sum wasted on his disastrous University career would have come in very useful.

" Yes," replied Jack, " it seems pretty considerable 'rot' to play the fool as we did last night ; but that is past and over. After all you weren't caught. What is the good of crying out before you're hurt ? Nobody saw you fellows get out of the window, so no one knows who was here last night."

" But we can't let you bear the brunt of it all. It was all my fault, how I was such a fool I can't make out. You mustn't suffer for me."

" Anyhow I have to suffer for myself, and have about earned the extreme penalty of University law. So I'd better be the only victim," said Jack mournfully, and then putting on a battered cap and a ragged gown he started off to interview his tutor, Mr. Perker.

CHAPTER IV.

A SYMPATHETIC COLLEGE TUTOR.

THE Reverend Edward Perker—or Teddy Perker as he was irreverently called by undergraduates—was the senior tutor of St. George's. He had not been born with a silver spoon in his mouth, for he was the son of a small tradesman at Cambridge, who had never succeeded in making more than a bare living out of his shop. Nor had Nature been very bountiful to him in the matter of personal gifts. He had a yellow bilious face, no particular features, and a strong cast in his little dyspeptic eyes. But better than being born rich or handsome he had been born lucky. He had tolerable brains too, though he was always an example, among his contemporaries, of a man who made a comparatively small amount of learning go as far as possible in obtaining University successes. At the Town Grammar School, where he was educated, he was an unpleasant little boy, with a taste for telling tales of his school-fellows. In consequence he was never tempted away from his lessons by other boys wishing to play with him. In due time he went up for a sizarship at St. George's, and just won it. He stuck to his books at college for much the same reason he did at school, and he was rewarded by taking a fair degree half-way up among the wranglers. Any other year he would not have got a fellowship, but here his luck came in. St. George's had unusually few good men that year. After fellowship he found what became the pursuit of his life. He took private pupils, and one long vacation, he was asked to stay at the country house of one of them. At the "Fellows" table he had never found it easy to make a favourable impression on his companions, or to find any subject on which he could shine in conversation. But at the country house there was one object on which he could interest his hostess, one of the proudest women in England. He could talk about her son.

Before that he had hated all undergraduates, for he always believed they were sneering at him and his low birth. Now he began to love them, or rather a section of them—as the Cambridge money-

lenders and dog-fanciers did—for what
he could get out of them. The men at
the high table of St. George's might
sneer at him, but people in the great
world would tolerate him, if he made himself useful to their sons. By good luck
he became one of the tutors of St.
George's, and in time senior tutor. His
side was always most popular with young
men of position and wealth. Great ladies
spoke of him with affection. Their sons
would always find a kind friend in Mr.
Perker. In fact sprigs of the nobility
who wished to live their own lives without troubling themselves much about
college discipline, could not find a more
complacent tutor. He tolerated poor
men who read hard, and were likely to
take good degrees, but men who were
poor, idle and had no influential relations
who could ask him to their country houses
in the vacation, were, he considered,
quite out of place at St. George's. Probably he was not far wrong, for the idle
poor man does not do much good at
the University. For Jack Warleigh,
Mr. Perker had at an early period of
their acquaintance conceived a great
dislike. Here was a young man who
had not much more than two hundred
a year to live upon at Cambridge, and he

gave himself airs, as if he were the eldest son of a nobleman. He detected too, a tendency on the young fellow's part to laugh at him. It was true Jack was the cousin of Sir George Warleigh, his very esteemed friend and old pupil, but when Mr. Perker had mentioned his name to Sir George, at a country house where they were staying, the baronet's manner had given him to understand that he did not take the slightest interest in his young kinsman, and had no very high opinion of him. Mr. Perker was only too willing to adopt that opinion. There was little love lost between them. Jack at first thought him a cadaverous-looking little wretch, with a manner full of distrust of himself and suspicions of other people ; and troubled himself very little about him, but he afterwards began to dislike him most cordially. There was nothing Mr. Perker resented more than to be despised by any one who had no position. At first he was inclined to believe that Jack must be somebody, but when he found out the facts of the case, he began to hate him, and to take care that he was duly punished for all his irregularities. It would have been impossible for him to have hated him, if he had been an eldest son with ten thousand a year, or even the younger son of any one of rank, for he honestly loved undergraduates of that class.

"Confound the little brute, he always wanted me 'sent down,' and now he'll have his way," Jack said to himself, as he climbed Mr. Perker's stairs.

"Hullo, Warleigh, going to see Teddy, are you?" said a young man, who passed him going down. "He's not a bad little chap," he added, in response to some maledictions which Jack growled out anent his tutor, "I've been overstaying my exeat by four days, but I got some game in Town, and said it was from the governor's place, and made up a message from the mater, saying she was looking forward so much to his paying a visit in the summer, and that put him all right."

"Yes, hang him, but I haven't a governor or a place to ask him to," Jack growled out, as he knocked at the door.

Once before, when he had been guilty of some trifling misdemeanour, Jack had found his tutor sitting at his table, with a piece of note paper before him.

"I was just writing to your mother, to ask her to have you removed from Cambridge," were the cheering words with which he was met on that occasion.

He expected a similar reception; "or perhaps," he thought, "now he has me at his mercy, he won't take the trouble to get up a piece of theatrical business."

Mr. Perker's rooms were artistically furnished with old oak, and there were some valuable prints on the walls, together with one or two dubious old masters about which their owner talked with a good display of art jargon; though of any real love of art he was as guiltless as when he was a grimy little boy at the Town Grammar School. Mr. Perker was standing before the fire, reading the *Times*, when Jack entered the room, and as he turned round to greet him, Jack noticed something in his face and manner which seemed to be intended to convey deep sympathy.

"Ah, Mr. Warleigh," he said, shaking his head and turning up his bilious little eyes; "this is a sad piece of news we have to-day, terribly sad!"

The big undergraduate looked at his little tutor with a gaze of rather sulky bewilderment.

"He seems to be taking a new line, considering that, once or twice, he has told me that it would end in my being 'sent down.' He need not pretend he is so astonished about it all," Jack thought to himself.

"Such a promising career cut short," Mr. Perker continued, with a sniff of commiseration.

"Well, if he thought my career promising, he kept it pretty much to himself. I believe the little beast is laughing at me," was Jack's inward comment, and he began to look savage, though he said nothing.

"Poor Sir George, he was one of the most promising young men we have had at St. George's. I had the greatest regard for him," continued Mr. Perker.

"If you mean my cousin, he doesn't care a rap about me, or I about him," said Jack, who was beginning to get out of patience.

"I know you don't mean to be unfeeling," Mr. Perker went on. "You probably did not understand each other. Why, have you not seen the sad news?" he added, as he noticed the expression of his pupil's face. "I must prepare you for a sad shock. Here is the paragraph," and taking up the *Times* from the table he pointed to a telegram from Scotland.

Jack Warleigh read that Sir George Warleigh's yacht, the *Sea Mew*, had been wrecked on the west coast. Sir George, his wife, and his two sons, had been on board, and all had been drowned.

His first emotion was that of sorrow. The difference it would make to his own life did not occur to him.

" Yes, it is terribly sad," he said, as he read it. " I never liked the little I knew of him, but I daresay he was a very good fellow in his way—distinguished and all that sort of thing." Then he read a paragraph underneath—the account of the wreck—which gave a biography of his cousin, and wound up with a statement which took his breath away, " The deceased baronet is succeeded in the title and family honours by Mr. John Warleigh, now a student at St. George's College, Cambridge." He had never thought of that.

Now that Jack had a title and a fine estate, no one could be more kind and sympathetic than Mr. Perker, and in a way his sympathy was genuine. He could now easily forgive Sir John his supposed insolence of manner and irregularities. Young men with titles and large incomes had a right, so he really thought, to be insolent and irregular.

There was another matter, about a disturbance in his rooms the night before, Mr. Perker went on to say. He had received a letter from the Junior Dean and the Proctor. It was very painful that it should have occurred at such a time. He had no wish to trouble him when he was suffering from so severe an affliction, but it might have to come before the masters and seniors, who would probably take a severe view of the case. However, Sir John could depend upon him doing his best for him. Under the circumstances, perhaps it would be as well if he went down for a few days. Anyhow, he would not come into residence again that term; but he hoped he would come up again and take his degree.

"Rum little chap, Teddy Perker, but not so bad as I thought him to be. After all, my change of fortune can make very little difference to him. He is not going to ask me to lend him any money. Really, he is very kind and considerate," Jack thought to himself, and he left his tutor's room in a very different frame of mind from that in which he entered it.

The folly of the night before, which had seemed so disastrous, had faded away, and most of Jack's remorse had flown also. He had never thought of stepping into dead men's shoes or counted the lives between himself and the entail, and he was honestly grieved for the sad fate of Sir George and his two sons, "poor little beggars," he said to himself; for all that his life had altered a good deal, and the alternative was certainly a pleasant one.

When he got back to his rooms, he found a visitor sitting on the one piece of furniture he had left, his table.

Mrs. Gruppy who had returned to do out the rooms, was entertaining him with a long and dismal account of her master's disaster, with an occasional excursion on Jack's character and goings on.

" All right, my good woman, you needn't stay here to talk to me, you may go, I'll wait for him," said the gentleman on the table, as he looked into a pocket book, the contents of which—it was a betting book—related to the recent week's racing at Newmarket, and seemed to afford a text for a good deal of thought.

" Well, Jack, how are you? this ancient servitor of yours has been talking me very nearly silly, about the mess you are in, which seems to be very serious, but perhaps this news will tend to mitigate it. I was staying at Newmarket for the week, with Hardborough, and when I heard of this, I thought that I'd stop here on my way, and look you up. We might go up to town together. We shall have to go down to Warleigh in a day or two," he said, as he got up from the table to shake hands with Jack.

"You remember me, don't you?" I am—let's see—your uncle, Cecil Warleigh."

The two were not unlike, but the elder was slighter, and a good many people would have said "better looking," for there was a singular charm in his face. At first sight one might almost call him effeminate looking, as one remarked his delicately cut features, soft wavy brown hair, and carefully trained moustache. But the look in his eyes showed that he had plenty of resolution and pluck, while his figure, though it was slight, was wiry and bespoke activity and strength. There was something about his appearance which suggested the notion that he was a horseman. It would be difficult to say what it was ; certainly his dress was free from any suspicion of horseyness, but the suggestion was there, none the less, and it was not belied by the fact, for Captain Warleigh was, so many good judges averred, the best gentleman rider of his day, both on the flat and across country.

"Let's see, why, it's about four years since we met at Fetchester," said Captain Warleigh, after Jack had declared that he remembered him perfectly well. "I little thought I was entertaining the head of the family, or that George and his two boys would go and leave you to succeed."

" I'm afraid I shan't make as satisfactory a head of the family as he was," said Jack.

" Don't know so much about that. Poor fellow, he is dead and gone now, and I daresay he was a very useful man, and all that sort of thing, but personally I thought him an infernal prig ; a sort of fellow out of whom you could never get anything but advice. Not that he knew more about me and my affairs than a child of seven. Yet one doesn't take the advice very well from one's nephew, although he was pretty nearly my own age."

" How about starting for town ? Have you to get leave ? or anything of that sort, for there is a train in an hour."

Jack said he had got leave, and was ready to start ; the sooner the better, he thought.

In an hour or so, uncle and nephew were both comfortably seated in the train, bound for London.

As Jack smoked a capital cigar, and listened to his uncle's talk about hunting, racing, and the life he would lead now he had become a rich man, he began to realize that the tragedy on the West Coast of Scotland would make his life very different, and no doubt a good deal jollier.

What a capital good fellow his uncle was, he thought.

He had always had a pleasant impression of him since that dinner at the "Swan" at Fetchester, and now he liked him better than ever. Cecil Warleigh for his part felt fairly contented with things as they were. Of course it would have suited him better if Jack hadn't been alive to stand in his way; but he was far too sensible a man to quarrel with any one for being born.

"And all said and done, he's a decided change from George, and a good deal more can be made of him," he thought, as he watched his nephew's young face light up at a story of a close finish he had made at Liverpool.

CHAPTER V.

CECIL WARLEIGH BEHAVES NICELY.

On their arrival in town Cecil and Jack Warleigh dined quietly at the latter's club. It would be better form under the circumstances, Cecil had suggested.

"Poor old George," said Cecil, as they smoked after dinner. "One ought not to say anything against him, but he was a fellow I never could get on with. As soon as the governor died he sent all the horses to Tattersall's, and gave Ring notice to quit Windmill Lodge, the neatest private training establishment for steeple-chasers in England. Now, the place is going to ruin, and hasn't had a tenant these five years."

"If I could afford it," said Jack, "I should like to have a horse or two in training. I remember very well the day you won the Grand National, on my grandfather's horse 'the Kipper;' and very proud I was of it, though I had

never seen you on the horse. I put on
ten shillings at the odds for the honour
of the family, and won ten pounds."

"Yes, that was my first Grand
National, I have won it once since then,
riding for Bamborough, but I'd like to
win it again in the Warleigh colours—the
old red and black stripes ; and I don't see
why I shouldn't, if you like to go in for it.
Ring would come back again to Windmill
Lodge, and there never was a better time
for getting a string of chasers together,"
answered Cecil, and he went into a
dissertation on the capabilities of Windmill Lodge, and the cost of having its
stables full again. "It was a shame
for a Warleigh of Warleigh not to have
some horses in training."

"I don't deny that it would have been
a very good thing for us, if the black and
red stripes had never been seen on a race-
course ; for the governor must have lost
a fortune in the old days," Cecil continued ; "but latterly, when he stuck
pretty much to chasing, he had a fair run
of success."

Now and then Jack would think of the
terrible accident on the West Coast of
Scotland, and of the father, mother, and
sons, who had all gone down together.
He felt half ashamed of himself for look-

ing forward with such keen relish to the change in his life which that calamity assured to him. George Warleigh had seemed to him cold and uncongenial, but he would have filled his place, and done his duty in life, well enough ; probably much better than he would. Cecil War- leigh, however, was not inclined to be very sympathetic when Jack talked in such a strain.

" Of course, my boy, you'll do your duty and all that sort of thing, well enough, and you'll find that a man with a good estate has far more influence in the county if he goes in for sport, it'll prejudice people in your favour. Poor old George would lecture in the village school-room, about all sorts of rot, and make long-winded speeches on politics, by the yard, which no one ever made head or tail of, as he hemmed and hawed through them. The governor had treble as much influence."

Having finished their cigars, Cecil suggested that perhaps as his last night had been such a late one, Jack had better turn in early, for his part he had to go round to another club to see a man.

" Last night," thought Jack, " why it seemed an age since that rowdy supper party—or since he had woke up that morning, trembling to think of having to face Mr. Perker." He was too excited to feel tired, but as Cecil did not appear anxious for his company, he would walk round to a college friend's lodgings, in Bury Street, where there was a spare bed-room for him. They parted at the corner.

"Precious lucky thing I was civil to that youngster the day the regiment came through Fetchester. There's nothing like making a good impression. Now he will be able to return the compliment," Cecil said to himself as he watched his nephew walking away. "Well, there's no good bringing him with me to-night, he will get there soon enough, on his own account, if he has a taste that way; besides it would not look well. As for me, every one knows that no one's death—except my own—would keep me from having a gamble, after such a bad week at Newmarket, so long as I have a penny to play with."

CHAPTER VI.

A NIGHT AND A MORNING.

THE club at which Cecil Warleigh determined to give fortune a chance of making up for lost time was a peculiar institution. At that time it was in full swing, though since, its career had been checkered. It was a most innocent and gloomy-looking place, but with all the outward appearance of a well-conducted club. In fact, for a short time it had been one of the mushroom growths which spring up all over London, having no particular characteristic except that from the first it was very unsuccessful. Then being turned into a temple to the Goddess of Fortune, it became more gloomy than ever in the day time, but at night it brightened up wonderfully. It was said that one member who had been transferred to it from some other proprietary club which had come to an untimely end— for a long time never discovered its *raison-d'être*, and would marvel as to how the few members who were to be seen in its deserted coffee and smoking rooms could possibly keep it going ; he used to come to the club at six and leave it at eleven. He made no acquaintance, in fact as a rule there was nobody there. One morning he read in a newspaper an account of an action brought on a cheque ; the defence being that it had been given for a gambling debt. There was a whole column of evidence about his club, and a sensational leader on the subject. Then he learned the secret of the club. The establishment slept until midnight, then woke up as a fashionable gambling-place.

Some years ago, those pleasant moralists whose favourite pursuit is to contrast our manners with those of our grandfathers, and point out how much we are improved, used to be very eloquent on the subject of Crockford's. The wicked hazard of the last generation had become a thing of the past, they used to boast. But there have been some interesting stories told in the Law Courts since those days, and it has become pretty evident that baccarat has taken the place of hazard, and within a stone's throw from what is now the Devonshire Club and once was that famous haunt of the

Goddess Fortune, there are the smaller and less celebrated establishments, which differ from it mainly in that the company is more mixed and the proprietorship less reputable.

In the card-room Cecil Warleigh found plenty of the gilded youth, many of whom he had met the day before at Newmarket, and they, like himself, were determined to do something to retrieve the bad past. There was a nobleman in there with large rent-rolls and income ; another nobleman whose rent-rolls found their way into the possession of trusts for his creditors ; a third with no rent-roll at all. There was a treasury clerk, who somehow lived, gambled, hunted, went everywhere on his pay and a hundred a year. There was a tremendous speculator on the Stock Exchange, who sixteen months before was at Dinan, in Brittany, without a penny to pay his hotel bill, hanging about the *poste restante*, waiting for an answer to any one of the many begging letters he had dispatched, and receiving nothing but indignant epistles from some of the more sanguine of his creditors. Now, his was the master mind of the alliance which " cornered " tin, and, strange to say, he found gambling at night a relaxation, after dealing in tens of thousands all day

in the city. There were one or two
members whose social standing were not
so well defined, a dark olive-faced gentleman who had been a clerk in a money-
changer's office at Malta, and—so some
one had declared—had been a croupier at
Monte Carlo, and had been dismissed for
dishonesty. He played boldly enough,
however, and paid when he lost, so no
one troubled about his previous history.
There were gentlemen who called themselves, Montague Lascelle and Lewis,
but whose names might have been Moses,
Lazarus and Levi, to judge from their
features. There were many other curious
specimens of the sharp on the rise, who
is so often to be found at this class of
club. The gentleman who has once gone
wrong, never gets back, but the sharper
and scoundrel does not find it so hard to get
up. Cecil Warleigh, however, troubled
himself but little as to who were there,
but settled himself down to play. He
had some two hundred pounds at his bank,
all that was left of the ten thousand
he had come into about five years before,
at his father's death. His losses at Newmarket amounted to five times as much,
and he vowed to himself that before he
went to bed that remnant of his patrimony
should be multiplied by five, or follow the

rest. For once it seemed that he was to be a gainer by so easily giving way to the tempter. He won stake after stake. He was worth four hundred, then six, then eight, nine—then the tide of fortune ebbed : now he was worth but seven, varying luck presently carried him on a second time to nine hundred. He got impatient, increased his stake, vowing to himself that he *would* reach the thousand pounds. Fortune seemed to be equally tired of playing with him. He lost—increased his stake again—again he lost. He now had but six hundred, now five, now but three, two, one. His capital grew smaller and smaller, as he played on with decreasing stakes, till the last sovereign flickered away like the flame from the end of a burnt stick. As he undressed that night, he realized that three sovereigns and a few half-crowns which he had in his pocket represented all his available capital.

Cecil Warleigh looked haggard and worn when he came into the breakfast-room the next morning. An evil-looking selection of letters had come by that morning's post, most of them he had left unopened, but the half-concealed venom about one envelope fascinated him, and he opened it to find, as he expected, the missive of a money-lender who evidently meant mischief.

"Well," he thought, "it was perhaps just as well that they had come; he would have it out with Jack at once, and see what he was willing to do for him."

"You're beginning your career just as I am finishing mine. Another week or two will see the last of me in England," Cecil said as he crumpled up the letter and bill, throwing them into the fire. "I'm dead broke—I should have been all right only they scratched Marmora for the Cambridgeshire, on the morning of the race, when she was at sixes; I'd taken on tens, and I was going to 'lay off,' when the first thing I hear in the morning is that she had broken down." This explanation was made by way of an excuse, for Cecil was by no means sure that his nephew might not be taken rather aback at the notion of his incurring debts of honour when he had no funds to meet them with. Jack, however, was so pleased that he could help Cecil, that he did not give the question of how he had got into debt much consideration.

"Remember I am 'Head of the family,' and if I can be of any use, I am only too glad. I suppose George would have done something, if he had been alive?"

"Well, yes, I suppose he would," agreed Cecil, who was by no means so certain of it in his own mind. "But he would have made an awful bother about it, and not taken it as you do. You are awfully good, and I am not likely to forget you have saved me from disgrace, perhaps utter ruin."

Then Jack said, as he was going to see the family lawyer that morning, he'd speak to him about raising the money. Then they went into figures; Cecil tentatively naming a sum, as the probable amount of his indebtedness, which, though it amounted to little more than half of what he really owed, somewhat surprised the nephew. Twenty-four hours before he had felt wretched because he owed about a hundred at Cambridge, now he was talking about paying thousands for his uncle.

"Don't know that I have ever thought about it before, but it seems to me to be a bit hard that the elder brothers should have thousands a year, and the younger brother not as many hundreds. I don't say it's not all right, and I know it is the law of entail that keeps properties together and makes England what she is, and all that sort of thing; but it does seem a little hard," said Jack simply.

"Well, my boy, it's very good of you to look at it like that, most elder sons think differently, and I don't know that I have much cause to grumble. It's a deuced deal better to be the son of a man with a landed estate, even if one is only a younger son, than the son of a man who never had a rap. And that's what it would have been, I suppose, if the land had always been cut up and divided. There have been a good many Warleighs who would have had their cut in at the property before our time. Of course it would have suited my book all the better if you'd been my niece instead of my nephew, old fellow, but I can't quarrel with you for that, at least I should be a fool if I did," Cecil answered, in that bright, pleasant manner of his, that had helped so much to make him so generally popular.

Jack Warleigh thought what a good fellow his uncle was.

Cecil Warleigh congratulated himself upon the "change for the better" in the headship of his family.

"You'll find old Grimshaw, the lawyer, rather a dried-up sort of old chap. I never could get on with him," said Cecil, and he spoke from his heart, for he had had more than one interview with the lawyer on the subject of money.

Just then a visitor was shown into the room. He was a man probably of about fifty years of age, but he had a youthful look about him, though his hair and moustache were quite white.

"I knew your father very well. We were great friends some thirty years ago," he said, as he shook hands with Jack, after he had been introduced as General Cottingham. Then, after having said a word or two about the wreck and Sir George Warleigh's death, he changed the conversation and began to chat about Newmarket.

"It's been a bad week for a good many of them. It finished young Flutterby. His horses are all to be sold, I hear," said the General.

"There are two or three of them that I wouldn't mind buying. He has got the only two steeplechase horses in training, in my opinion, and one or two of his two-year-olds are very smart," said Cecil, and then he looked thoughtfully at Jack for a minute or two. "Why shouldn't you buy them? If one of 'em isn't the winner of a Grand National, I'm much mistaken," he continued.

"Ah! I'm afraid you'll find him a very dangerous adviser, he knows everything, but somehow always comes to grief," said the General.

"I think you'll admit when I have ridden a horse—and I have ridden both of Flutterby's—I know something about them," put in Cecil.

"Well, Cecil," said the General, after Jack had taken his departure, "how about Newmarket? Some kind friends are wondering whether your account will be settled next Monday?"

"That is one's friends all over; but they'll find themselves wrong this time," answered Cecil Warleigh pleasantly enough, "I don't mind telling you," he said, "that I should have been in rather a tight place, if it hadn't been for that youngster who has just gone out. He has behaved like a brick about it."

"All's well, that ends well, I suppose; but if the *Sea Mew* hadn't gone down? A defaulter is rather an ugly-sounding name. Take my advice, and let this be a warning to you, though I don't want to preach."

"I was twelve hundred to the bad, but plenty of fellows owe the bookmakers twice that amount."

"I daresay there are some book-makers who would be glad enough to let you owe them more than that. Steeple-chasing isn't what it was. Still, a man who rides as many favourites as you do, in the course of a winter, might do 'em a pretty good turn. I saw poor old Flamby to-day, he borrowed a few shillings from me. There was never much harm in poor Flamby, but see what he has come to."

" You're right, General, he seemed to go wrong all at once. Took to riding for the biggest gang of thieves on the turf, and being hand and glove with 'em in all their robberies."

" He began by owing money in the ring, though," said the General, unpleasantly harking back to the subject. The General was the only man who ever ventured to give Cecil Warleigh advice. Cecil was one of the most popular men in the service, though perhaps he was liked a little better out of his regiment than in it.

General Cottingham, however, who had been Colonel of his regiment, was the best friend he had. He knew him better than other men did, and had formed an estimate of his character which was less flattering than that generally current. For all that, he was indulgent to the faults he saw so clearly. It was his custom to measure conduct by what he felt he might do himself, under certain circumstances, and, looking back, he could remember very few occasions when he had not yielded to temptation. He had a pleasantly cynical toleration which assisted him in finding out the weak points in a man's character, and made him a model confessor, never being too shocked to give excellent advice.

"No man can say anything against me," Cecil answered, without showing any resentment.

"No, I believe you, and I hope they never will, but you for the future take my advice, and do not back your ill-luck so wildly, when you're having a bad race-meeting. That young fellow who has just gone out may be a very good sort of youngster, but sooner or later—rather *sooner* than *later*—he will get tired of settling your debts. There are plenty of good fellows with properties, but there isn't one of them, that I know, who shares with any of his impecunious relatives."

"Let's change the subject, General, and talk of something pleasanter, what do you think of the Liverpool Cup?"

"Well, I'm afraid I must be off," said the General, "but if you are not better or worse employed this evening, come and dine, and bring your nephew, and we'll have a look over the entries."

CHAPTER VII.

JACK WARLEIGH BEGINS TO LIVE.

At Lincoln's Inn, Jack Warleigh, after he had heard all the details of the loss of the *Sea Mew*, and the arrangements which had been made for the funerals of Sir George and his sons, went into the question of paying Cecil's debts.

Old Grimshaw, the lawyer, looked uncommonly dry when he heard this suggestion. "It is not my business, perhaps, to give you advice as to how you should spend your money, Sir John," he remarked, "but I think I ought to tell you that the property won't stand too much of that sort of thing. It is not what it was. Six thousand a year is nearer the figure than ten thousand, nowadays; and Captain Warleigh," here the old lawyer hesitated, and looked lovingly at the Warleigh deed boxes on his shelves.

"I'm sure my uncle is a very good fellow," put in Jack.

"I believe that Captain Warleigh is a perfectly charming young man ; but one way or another he has spent more money on his amusements than would have been prudent if he had been an *elder* son.   His father paid his debts again and again, and left him all he could when he died. He has had a fair share out of the estates," and again the old man's eyes wandered to the tin boxes, which probably contained documentary evidence of Cecil's doings.

Jack Warleigh troubled himself very little about the encumbrances on the estates.   He was only twenty-one, and had owned the property but twenty-four hours.

"Well, the money must be forthcoming, somehow or the other," said Jack, "for I promised Cecil to get it for him ; and for the future, I think something ought to be settled.   What will he do for money?"

"Pretty much the same as other people do, who have spent all they had. Still, perhaps it would be cheaper in the end if you, once for all, did whatever you are going to do.   There is no end to paying debts," answered Mr. Grimshaw, and then added that the money would be forthcoming.   But he took care to show by his manner that he thoroughly disapproved of the proceeding.

"It is no good saying anything, Jack, but you must know how I feel. I shan't forget your generosity," said Cecil, when they met in the evening, ready to start for General Cottingham's. Undoubtedly he did feel grateful. If there had to be some one standing in his light, there certainly could not be a better fellow for the position than Jack.

"Is there a Mrs. Cottingham?" asked Jack, as they were driven down to Kensington in a hansom.

"No, she died years ago. She was a Miss Kate Clifford, a celebrated actress Cottingham ran away with, and married her after she was divorced. He behaved well enough about it, in a way; but it caused a quarrel with his people, and spoilt his career, for a black mark against one's name helps no one. And this, to a certain extent, prevented him getting on in the service, beyond commanding the regiment."

"And what is the daughter like?"

"Oh, she's about twenty-three, but I have not seen her for three years, and we shall both see her in five minutes," said Cecil.

A tall, slight girl, with a mass of dark wavy hair, a singularly colourless face, with rather a large nose, a finely shaped and delicately cut mouth, was the first impression Jack formed of Kate Cottingham. He noticed also the long and well-shaped hand she held out to him, as also a somewhat repellent manner, as she shook hands with Cecil Warleigh. He found himself talking a good deal to her, at dinner and afterwards, while Cecil chatted with the General about soldiering, racing, and hunting.

They had sat down to dinner at about half-past-eight, so the evening was not a long one, but before it was over, Jack had learned to know those blue-grey eyes, that now and again from under their long lashes would sparkle with fun and mischief, though when in repose there was a sad, yearning expression in them. Once, when she was singing at the piano, and Cecil was leaning over her, talking, Jack thought they looked hard and reckless; but he forgot the impression so soon as she began to talk with him again. She had none of that bright beauty that dazzles and charms at the first glance; hers was a face you might not be struck by, but if you tried to read it, you would find it haunting you.

Jack had seldom met with any one to whom he could talk so easily. He told her a good deal about himself, and described how the news of his cousin's death had come to him.

"Poor fellow!" he was saying, "when I first heard of the accident, I thought how sad and terrible it was; and now I only seem to think of the difference it makes to me. I wonder if I heard that it was a mistake, and that he had not been drowned, whether I should be sorry or glad?"

"The most we can do is not to wish people dead, in such cases; I met him once or twice, but we never got on together. His kind of man never likes me much, I think," was Miss Cottingham's remark. "I thought him rather a muff."

"Poor George Warleigh gave me just that impression. But what sort of people do you mean don't like you?"

"Very good, respectable people. You see, they think my existence a mistake, and my bringing up an outrage. I suppose it is not very conventional; I was left to run wild about the barracks, with no one to look after me; but, after all, I did not get into such very great mischief. Tell me, how long have you known Captain Warleigh? I do not remember that he ever talked of you."

"I suppose not, I only met him once before yesterday. That was when I was

at school; his regiment came through
Fetchester, but from that day I've
thought him the finest fellow in the
world."

"Yes," she replied, "I suppose as a
boy you would think so. One loses one's
enthusiasm as one gets older." For a
second her eyes were fixed on Cecil, who
was talking to her father. Then she
changed the conversation to some other
subject.

Uncle and nephew walked back to St.
James's in silence.

Jack's thoughts wandered back to old
days, and then came round to Kate
Cottingham's blue-grey eyes. He had
never lived until that day, he thought.

"Grey eyes go to Paradise," he said, re-
peating aloud a French phrase which he
had read somewhere in a novel. His accent
showed a classical education, and perhaps
on that account Cecil understood it all the
easier.

"Eh, do they! well, they have sent a
good many men to the other place," he
interrupted, and Jack blushed and looked
confused at being overheard.

That night as they smoked, before
going to bed, Cecil was singularly taciturn,
and helped himself more liberally than
was his wont to whiskey.

CHAPTER VIII.

MR. PARADINE DROPS HIS CANE.

FROM year to year, little enough happens in a sleepy old town like Fetchester; boys leave the school, and others take their places, and follow in their footsteps. Ideas about education change, but for all that, boys grow up into much the same sort of men, with much the same sort of vices and virtues which distinguished their fathers, who had not the advantage of being educated by masters of the modern school, to whom there has been given a revelation as to boy nature.

At Fetchester, interest centres round what Mr. Chadband calls the human boy; the parents who have come to the place for his schooling, being mere appendages, as are the healthy friends of invalids at a German Spa. Conversation turns on Bobby's canings, and Billy's prizes, on the headmaster's jokes, and the junior master's eccentricities. They talk 'boy'

at Fetchester, as they talk 'horse' at
Newmarket; the schoolmaster being
looked up to with awe and reverence,
even by mature human beings.

But in Fetchester, as elsewhere, there
come eras of change, and such a time
was preceded by two events; one of
which was discussed eagerly, for its
personal interest, though it did not affect
the town, or its people. The other event
seemed to divide ancient Fetchester
history from modern.

The first was Jack Warleigh's succession to the family estates and
honours. Fetchester had plenty to say
about it, taking a great interest in the
future of the gentle widow lady and her
son. There was much debate as to
whether she would go away and live at
Warleigh, her son's house, or stay on
at Fetchester, and people who hardly
knew her by sight discussed the subject,
as local news is discussed in such a place.
To the disgust of superior people, who
love to preach to their fellow-men an
endless sermon about themselves and
their opinions, and boast that they take
no interest in petty personal gossip, Mrs.
Warleigh was unwilling to leave
Fetchester. The place was endeared to
her by almost all the tender memories of

her life. Its quiet had helped to soothe
the sorrows of her widowhood. Warleigh
had been her husband's old home, but
she had never set foot in the house. It
was at Fetchester that she first saw him,
and it was at Fetchester that she came
back after his death. So, when the
change came in her son's fortune, she did
not give up the little house they had
always lived in, but still kept it as her
home, though she consented to spend a
good many months of the year at Warleigh.

Nelly Paradine, when she heard of the
change in Jack's life, had a very heavy
heart. Some people noticed her looking
out of spirits, and those who were ill-
natured, said she was annoyed to think
how badly she had played her cards.

To tell the truth, she never thought
once of having missed becoming the
mistress of Warleigh Hall; but it seemed
to her that the determination she had
formed a few days before to beg Jack's
forgiveness must be put away for ever,
she could not make up her quarrel now.

Another Fetchester event happened
some ten weeks after the great change
in Jack Warleigh's fortunes. An afternoon came that Fetchester boys who
were in Mr. Paradine's class will not

forget. The old master had been unusually soft and gentle that day. It now
and then was his custom to illustrate the
classical author that happened to be the
subject of the lesson, by bringing out
from his desk some well-worn volume of
English poetry and reading lines from
his favourite authors that dealt with
the same ideas. Some of the boys learnt
from those readings a love of good
English literature. The idle ones
rejoiced greatly when they saw those
books come out, for they hoped that the
cane would rest, and a blessed calm take
the place of that stormy half hour when
the boys at the bottom of the class had
to try their hands at parsing. That day
he had read from Pope for some time,
but he seemed to get tired, and, to the
dismay of the idle ones of the class, shut
up his book, and determined to go on
with the construing of Virgil. Bolderson,
a boy who sat some ten places from the
bottom of the class, was set to construe,
and the boys who sat below him prepared themselves for the fray. Bolderson would give them no chance. He was
a boy of colossal ignorance, and would
fail, probably, to construe one word, and
what he missed would be passed down
the class, and those below him would

have the chance of correcting his blunders. But the boys below him desired no opportunity for display, they were perfectly content with their places, and only asked to be let alone. Besides they knew but little more than the unhappy Bolderson, and believed that they were destined to share his ignominy, and, what was of more account to them, his punishment. Bolderson also would take shots, and his shots had a peculiarly galling effect upon the scholarly ear of Mr. Paradine. That day he read some half-dozen lines of Latin, making one or two false quantities; they did not, however, arouse the master's ire, he had leaned back in his chair and thrown a handkerchief over his eyes, and had let his cane drop on to the floor. The unhappy boy, for a second or two, stared blankly at the Latin lines he had read, and then dashed wildly at them. The boys at the top of the class tittered a little at the rendering of those lines, for which Bolderson, who was a heavy-fisted boy, scowled vengeance. His translation became more and more wild, and all waited for the outburst. But no sound came from Mr. Paradine. Bolderson looked at the master warily, and his voice subsided into a hum, then ceased altogether, and he stole back to his seat. The class at first kept silence. The maxim that tells one to "let sleeping dogs lie" seemed to apply. Then some of the bolder spirits began to move. One of them pretended to throw a book at the master, another to play with his cane. Bolderson, who had always a peculiar reading of a joke, crept up to where one of the boys who had laughed at him sat, and stuck a steel pen into him. The boy cried out sharply, but his cry did not wake up Mr. Paradine. Then gradually the boys began to realize that something was wrong. The grins faded away from their faces, and they became awe-struck and frightened. One of them went to a master in the next room, he came, and after he had looked at the figure in the chair, at once dismissed the class. The boys went away quietly and gravely, and spoke to each other with bated breath. A doctor was sent for, but before he arrived most of the boys knew that they had seen death. Men of the modern school, who talk new-fangled nonsense about corporal punishment, would have been surprised to have heard how the boys talked of their good old friend, · whose voice, often enough raised angrily, they had heard for the last time. There was a rugged kindliness and humour that made them like him; and perhaps some of those who seemed to have the kindliest memory of him were high-spirited idle boys who had most often been his subjects.

Nelly Paradine had always been the sunshine of her father's life, and at first she was numb with grief. But she telegraphed at once to Joe at Cambridge, and by searching among papers, discovered an address that would probably in time find out Sam the outcast. The two brothers, who had not seen each other since Joe was a boy of fifteen, met again. Joe, the Fellow of Cambridge, eyed his elder brother with considerable mistrust, and it was with the greatest difficulty that Sam could borrow a few shillings from him, so that he could make stealthy visits to the public houses he used in the old days, to make inquiries as to the welfare of the bygone race of barmaids.

Sam had not been at Fetchester for years, and he remembered what a very dashing youngster he was, in those past days, with what awe the boys of the school, and the young men at the " Swan," his old play-fellows, then regarded him. He did not spend much time there, in the days of his splendour; for Fetchester was dull then, and besides, when he was at home he somehow had felt most the sense of impending disaster, which, reckless as he was, was never wholly absent from him. After his smash he had spent some weeks there, and dreary enough they were. But he was a swell in those days, though a swell under a cloud. Now it was different; still, he wore his battered tall hat jauntily, and made the best of the obviously unkind present. He was not without remorse, for he knew that his escapades had broken his father's life and most likely helped to cut it short. His brother Joe, who was some three years his junior, and had once upon a time felt very jealous of him, rather enjoyed the position, during the few sad days before the funeral, of being able to lecture his elder brother. Sam took the lecturing meekly enough.

"After all, Joe, there's not much use in dwelling upon it all. Let the dead past bury its dead. Let us look at things as they are. You are in comfort and affluence. Now, I am not going to ask you for anything for myself, but what are we going to do for Nelly? I don't suppose the poor old governor has left anything."

"You have good reason to know that, Samuel, and to know what happened to the savings of his life-time."

" Perhaps I have, Joe, but that doesn't answer the question. What are we going to do for Nelly ? "

" *We*," repeated Joe with an unpleasant emphasis, " what do *you* propose doing ? "

" Well, when things look up a bit, I intend to see she doesn't want. At present the question rests with you, what can you give her ? "

" I have given her advice. I have told her that circumstanced as she is, she will be far happier earning her own living and being independent. Lots of girls, nowadays, have to do it, and it really is no hardship at all for her."

" If you had my experience, you would know that it is a hard world to have to fight against. Advice, Joseph, my boy; however good it is, in this case is worth about just what it costs to give it. If you won't do anything for her, she'll have to earn her living," said Sam.

When the funeral was over, it was found that there was nothing left but a few debts. The day after it, Nelly received a visit from Mrs. Warleigh, who, when she heard of her trouble, forgot the unkindness between them. Nelly must " come and live with her. She was all by herself, a great deal too much so, and she wanted a companion."

Mrs. Warleigh's friendship seemed sweeter than ever it had been ; but Nelly recognized at once that the offer could not be accepted. She could not live in Jack Warleigh's house, or constantly see him, as she would be bound to do, if she lived with his mother. So the refuge which the widow had offered was lost to her. It was finally arranged that she was to stay with some friends who lived in the town, until she could procure a situation as governess or companion. Joseph, her brother, gave her more advice, and then hurried back to Cambridge, anxious to get away from sorrow and poor relations. Sam sighed at having to leave free lodgings and regular meals.

"Nelly," he said, as he took leave of his sister, and as he spoke he jingled together in his pocket the two sovereigns which with great difficulty he had managed to extract from his brother, "Joe is a mean beggar. One can't expect much from à Cambridge small-college man—Sam felt the dignity of having been 'sent down' from Christ-church—but though he is my brother, I cannot help owning that Joe is, I should say rather below than above the form of his college. I never could get anything out of him—that is an old story—but he ought to do something for you."

Nelly answered readily enough that she did not wish Joe to do anything of the kind; and that she was anxious to fight her own way in the world.

"Well, my dear," replied Sam, "I hope you'll find the world a kinder one to you than it has been to me. Things seem to be looking up though, just now, and it may be the time will come when I shall be able to make a home for you."

Sam was one of those men whom misfortune and poverty, somehow, seemed to swell. Like Falstaff they "blew him up;" and in his new black clothes and glossy hat, he really made quite an imposing appearance.

"In the meantime, my dear," he continued, "the kindest thing I can do is to keep out of your way."

Nelly did not build very much on that rather remote future when Sam would be of much assistance to her; still she found that she liked him, and that she thought less of his wickedness and extravagance than she used to in the days of his splendour.

So Nelly went to stay with her friends, and took to reading the advertisements in the papers and generally doing her best to find something to do ; feeling the truth of the advice tended to her by her brother Joseph, that she would be wise not to be too particular to begin with, as there were so many other girls in her position.

In a month or two a new master was appointed in place of Mr. Paradine—a Mr. Meek, a young man who disapproved of corporal punishment, and who had a lot of brand-new maxims for the proper treatment of his pupils. He seemed to believe that boys had only just been invented, that men before his time could have had no opportunity of learning anything about them.

The boys somehow despised him, knowing, with a boy's instinct, that he was a muff, albeit a well-meaning one. Old Par became a pleasant memory, and his canings were looked back to as experiences that it was creditable to have undergone.

CHAPTER IX.

THE FETCHESTER HUNT STEEPLE-CHASES.

IN the month of February, Fetchester was divided into two factions. Those who were opposed to, and those that were in favour of, the steeple-chase meeting, that was held some three miles from the town, and had become an annual fixture. The good folk of the little town took sides, and wrangled over the question as to whether or no steeple-chasing were a pernicious and demoralizing sport, and whether the meeting should be abolished or supported : quite oblivious to the fact that they had very little to do with it, one way or the other. The large majority of the townspeople were, however, in favour of the meeting, and look upon it as one of the red-letter days of their year. They regard not the fact that Gallows Hill farm is not an attractive spot on a chill February day, nor do they pay much heed to the warnings of the clergy of

all denominations; the Rev. Father
Latimer on this occasion, and on this
occasion only—holds out a hand as he
expresses it, to his dissenting brethren—
and the Church of England parsons and
the local Stigginses unite, as in a labour
of love, to preach the evils of racing.

The meeting that was held some sixteen months after Jack Warleigh came
into his property was doubly interesting
to some of the Fetchester people, from
the fact that he had lately purchased
several steeple-chasers, and was to
appear in the character of an owner for
the first time. Mr. Flutterby, whose
intention to sell his horses was reported
more than a year before, had managed
to last for another twelve months.
He had won the Grand National with his
horse the Crier, who beat Jack Sheppard
the favourite, much more easily than any
one knew, except Cecil Warleigh who
rode him.

The next season's flat-racing had
settled Mr. Flutterby, and after the
Liverpool Autumn races, his horses were
sold, and Sir John Warleigh became the
owner of Clovis and the Crier. They
were, so Cecil assured him, the two best
steeple-chasers in training; and with
them, and several other useful horses

which Cecil had purchased for him, the old prestige of Windmill Lodge as a training establishment was likely to return again. Tom Ring, the trainer, who had his stalls almost empty for the two years during which Sir George the younger reigned at Warleigh, was in high feather again. The lodge and stables, which had grown somewhat out of repair, were renovated, and in course of a little time looked quite spick-and-span.

Jack had spent most of his time since he came into his fortune rather sensibly than otherwise, for he had gone back to Cambridge and taken his degree. Down at Warleigh he had already become very popular.

The late baronet, whose untimely fate had been duly deplored, was, every one admitted, a very great loss. He was a good Conservative, and no doubt had a great career before him; but there was no denying that he was a wet blanket, and his praiseworthy wish to be always instructing his fellow-men was the cause of many a weary hour to his friends. Jack Warleigh seemed to them to be much better suited to ordinary every-day life. He was fond of out-door amusements, would, most likely, be ready to take the hounds and entertain his neighbours.

The fact that he was a bachelor, and, according to all reports, perfectly free from any engagement or entanglement, naturally increased the interest with which he was regarded.

People at Fetchester took a great interest in his doings. No longer were those in the majority who talked of him as one rapidly going to the dogs. Had not he taken his degree at Cambridge, which showed great industry and determination on his part, and, after all, what were the stories that they used to shrug their shoulders at, but mere signs of his vitality and natural high spirits.

" Now, by George ! he has the ball at his feet, and has nothing to do but enjoy himself," said old Major Chaffinch, when at his family breakfast. table he read that Jack had taken his degree.

" He will be able to do a great deal of good," answered the elder of the young Chaffinches, who was always trying to graft a moral on to his old father's not very edifying discourse.

" Well, I see he has bought Clovis and the Crier, and he means to run the former at our steeple-chase next week. It shall carry a pound or two of my money, for luck, and the sake of old times," continued the Major.

"Gambling—and all racing is gambling—is a degrading vice, inexcusable even in the young and rich," said the excellent young man, as he soberly ate his bread and butter. "I'm afraid Warleigh is likely to make but very little good use of his fortune."

"A pound or two of *your* money, did you say? I did not know that you had any money," was the pleasant remark with which Mrs. Chaffinch greeted her spouse's somewhat ill-timed burst of confidence. She was a fat, heavy woman, with a perpetual expression of martyrdom. She did not speak often; but when she did, it was to the purpose.

For all that, old Chaffinch did turn up at the steeple-chases, and took up his position on the drag of the Loyal Lancers, whose head-quarters were at Brilleton, the big manufacturing town some twenty miles away, and who had a detachment at Fetchester.

Loamshire is a county of small landowners, good sportsmen and cheery, pleasure-loving people, who support the steeple-chases, and there were a goodly array of carriages along the rails opposite the Stand, from a good many of which the soldiers' coach was regarded with special interest, for Jack Warleigh had come over in it, with Cecil, to see the latter, for the first time, ride in his colours— the famous red and black stripes, which in old Sir George's time were so celebrated both across country and on the flat. Such of the good people of Loamshire who had never seen him before were thoroughly well pleased with his appearance.

"Yes, he is quite a nice-looking young man!" said Lady Shoddyton, wife of Mr. Oldlands of Oldland, and widow of the late Sir Thomas Shoddyton, Governor of the Fly River Settlements, whose name and title she retained, as she inspected the officers' drag through her gold-rimmed eye-glasses; "and if he gets into good hands will suit us very well. But he looks weak, and I am afraid that his uncle, Captain Warleigh, is not a good companion for him. Who is that girl he is talking to? I don't know her. Where does she come from? That's the worst of soldiers, they encourage a very doubtful kind of society. Their wives are too often objectionable."

"Look at that old cat staring at us," said pretty Mrs. Burke, wife of Major Dick Burke of the Lancers, to Kate Cottingham, who had come down with her father from London, and was the object of

Lady Shoddyton's attention. "She doesn't approve of either of us. The old wretch hates every woman who has any looks to boast of. Her one object in life is to find husbands for her brood of nieces, who she passes off on the innocent squireens of Loamshire as girls of the bluest blood. After they're married, the husbands are introduced to her ladyship's brother, their father-in-law, a decayed West Indian merchant, who fuddles himself with rum, and whose identity is kept a dead secret in the family like the ghost of Bogie's Castle."

"She's a clever woman, my dear, and I respect her. I wish I had her talent, I'd sell a horse, when I had one to part with, instead of giving it away, as I do," put in Dick Burke, looking up from opening a bottle of champagne.

"I wish you had, Dick," answered his wife merrily.

"Yes, I'll give her her due, she is clever. Cecil, why don't you make your nephew go and swear allegiance?"

"She's not over-fond of me, is her ladyship. Don't think she likes the regiment either. We know too much for her," answered Cecil Warleigh, who had come across from the Stand to snatch a hurried luncheon. He spoke lightly enough, but he felt rather out of temper, for he was having a bad day ; and there was another matter just then to annoy him.

An unaccustomed flush came across Kate Cottingham's usually colourless face; she felt angry with her friend Mrs. Burke and the Lady of Oldlands. She was far more sensitive to slights than many would believe, who watched the bold way in which she carried herself. Owing to the circumstances of her birth, she had to a certain extent always found herself at war with society. She had never known what it was to be with womankind of her own blood, who could protect and make her feel on sure ground in society. That vulgar woman in the carriage probably would hear a whispered account of her birth and parentage, which would increase the insolence of her stare.

"Well, here's luck to the 'black and red stripes,'" said Dick Burke, as he held up a glass of champagne ; "may they be to the fore as often as they used to be in the old days, when they carried everything before them across country. Ah ! those were the palmy days of steeplechasing. There will never be another one like old Sir George Warleigh's Allegory, who won the Grand National three years in succession. They don't breed that class of horse nowadays."

"Don't be too sure of that, Major Burke, you'll admit that Tom Ring is a pretty good judge as to how good a mare Allegory was. Well, he tells me that I have a better one in the Crier. Clovis can't touch him, and yet I fancy you'll see to-day that he is not a bad horse. If I win to-day, the Crier's second Grand National ought to be a certainty," was Jack's prophetic answer.

"I am right glad to hear it, my boy, both for your sake and the honour of the regiment, for Cecil is going to ride, I take it," then noticing the expression with which Cecil was regarding Jack, he continued, "come, old chap, you needn't look so grumpy ; surely you won't grudge us a little information from your stable ? You surely wouldn't want to keep the regiment from backing your mount ?"

"Don't remember that you were so very anxious to see that we all had our money on, when you won the Grand Military last year," replied Cecil.

"'Deed, I would have been though, if I had thought that I should have done it. Many's the time I've seen you boys win your money, by one of my horses, and been as pleased, as about the bit I got for meself. No one in the regiment can say that I don't tell 'em when to put their money on me."

"No, Major, we can't," said a subaltern, mournfully remembering past losses.

"Ah, Sir John, you'll find out it's mighty little gratitude you get from the public for keeping horses in training for them to win their money on," said the Major to Jack, "but take my word for it, for all that, you won't be any the worse, in the long run, for letting your friends share in your good luck. Don't you agree with me, Bamborough?"

"Yaas, I think we're pretty much of a mind, Major. One's pals have other pals whom they tell, and they have others, and so on *ad infinitum*. So when I have a 'good thing,' I take particular care to tell my nearest and dearest just what I want Tom, Dick, and Harry to know. If you want to let any one at all in, you must first let in your friends," was Lord Bamborough's rejoinder.

Lord Bamborough was a big, red, bloated-looking young man, who was staring somewhat malevolently out of his prominent and bloodshot eyes at Jack Warleigh. Among men who did not know him very well, Lord Bamborough had the reputation of making himself out worse than he really was.

"Now let me drink success to your colours. I hope you'll win to-day, and

that you often will win," said Kate Cottingham to Jack. "I shall never get tired
of going to race meetings, so long as I can
see them in front, and I mean to make
a small fortune by backing them," she
continued.

"Then you may be sure that I'll have
a lot more horses in training. I have
nothing but steeple-chasers now; but
I'll buy some racers," said Jack, his face
lighting up with a pleasure he had never
experienced before.

"No," said Miss Cottingham, "promise
me you won't do that because of what
I was foolish enough to say. I know a
good deal about these things, and I know
how dangerous an amusement the turf is.
No, you must not do that. I like to see
my friends do well in other things besides
racing and sport. If I were you, I would
never be content until I had made a
career for myself. I would go into
politics and public life. Oh! you men,
how lucky you are! You can fight your
own way to the front. It seems that half
of you are not ambitious. Fancy not
being ambitious!"

"Kate is a very strong-minded young
woman, and professes a very lofty contempt for all us drones; though I will
say this for her—that she has never

become a senior wrangler, or a lady doctor, or a lady agitator on her own account," said General Cottingham, laughing.

"No, women only succeed in making themselves ridiculous. I am not fond of amusing other people by follies of that sort. But for men, it is different. However, for the present I hope Clovis will win to-day."

"That's unkind of you too, Miss Cottingham, considering I ride Bellman in the race. You won your money by backing one of mine in the first race," said Bamborough; then continuing, "and mind you, you are wrong too, for I am going to win."

Lord Bamborough knew as much about racing as most men; and on the flat he had the reputation of being one of the cleverest owners on the turf. He had one weakness that he would never admit. He could not ride a race himself. As a matter of fact, though, he had plenty of pluck. He had not an ounce of judgment. When the book-makers knew he was going to ride, the odds against his mount always increased.

"We had better get across to the Stand," said Cecil, looking extremely sulky. Then, as he climbed down from the drag, he whispered to Kate, " You're making the running pretty strongly with that youngster." She did not reply, but a quiver, as of pain, shot across her face, and turning round she began to talk to Lord Bamborough.

CHAPTER X.

THE FETCHESTER HUNT CUP.

NEVER had a man, thought Cecil Warleigh, better excuse than he had for feeling out of temper. He had not backed Bamborough's horse for the first race; as past experience had made him register a vow, never to have a penny on that nobleman's mount. Then, in the second race, a Military Stakes, for which he thought he was a certainty, he had just been beaten by a horse belonging to Major Burke. The Major pretended to be extremely surprised at having won the race.

"I'm getting an old man now, Cecil my boy, and shan't ride many more races, let alone win 'em. Sure you wouldn't grudge me a bit of luck like this?" said honest Dick Burke; but there was a sparkle in his eye, which told Cecil that it had not been such a surprise to him, and that he had won a good bit of money.

It was a confoundedly unfriendly thing keeping it so dark, and not letting him know how good it was.

In the third race—thanks to a good pair of glasses—he had seen the rider of the favourite—which he had backed—break a stirrup leather, and he was in time to get a big bet on the second favourite, for whom the race ought then to have been a certainty, if it had not—as it did the next minute—fallen at the brook. Altogether he was thoroughly out of temper. Never was he so convinced of Jack's being altogether a mistake, a person who never ought to have been in the world at all.

It was, to a certain extent, a consolation to have a definite grievance against him, on which he could enlarge.

"What on earth makes you talk all over the place, about what the Crier can do? We shall have the horse at some absurd price for Liverpool. Upon my word, it is sickening," said Cecil, speaking more bitterly than he usually did.

"Surely there was no harm, telling the men on the drag that I thought I had a good chance. There was hardly any one except the men of your regiment."

"Regiment! what the deuce does that matter? Burke is about the keenest hand on the turf, and Bamborough has a horse entered for the race, and yet you must chatter away like a boy."

"Well, if I choose, I don't see why I shouldn't let my friends know that I think I have a good chance, I hate having so much mystery about it."

"All right, tell every one you're bound to win, and you'll find that no one will thank you if you do win, and every one will howl at you if you don't. But it's your business, not mine, I suppose," growled Cecil, who was now thoroughly savage.

"Don't be riled, old fellow. I won't talk so much in future," Jack said good-humouredly, and Cecil, who began to feel his kinsman was getting out of leading-strings, and might perhaps with wisdom be humoured, made a more pleasant reply, saying Jack was too good a fellow, and that on the turf he would find wearing his heart on his sleeve rather a mistake. As they passed into the enclosure an incident happened which served to illustrate Cecil's remarks, and gave him further ground for complaint.

Lounging near the gate was a young man dressed in a very baggy white driving coat, with huge mother-of-pearl buttons. On his head he wore—much on one side

—a very curly brimmed brown billycock hat. The coat was thrown open, so as to disclose a tremendously loud suit of checks, and a heavy gold watch chain, which was probably attracting the attention of the swell mob. "Hullo, old chappie, you're become a great swell since we last parted. Do you remember that night in your rooms in St. George's? What a lark it was!" said the young gentleman, who was no other than Jack's Cambridge acquaintance, Mr. Raggles of Magdalen.

Jack remembered that once he had rather an admiration for Raggles, who was considered by his friends to be a very knowing, dashing man-of-the-worldish fellow. Either he or Jack had altered a great deal; for now Raggles seemed bad form and noisy.

"I say, is your horse going to win the Cup? Good enough for me to back, eh? And what about the Crier for Liverpool?"

"I think he'll win, but am not very sure about it. The Crier is a good bit the better of the two, and ought to win easily at Liverpool, unless we've made a big mistake."

"By Jove! Jack, you're too bad," said Cecil, as Mr. Raggles walked away with two men to whom he had been talking before he had seen Jack.

"He's an old college friend," Jack explained to Cecil.

"Then all I can say is, that your college friend has managed to pick up two of the biggest scoundrels on the turf, to associate with. On my word they turn out some fine specimens of the genus fool at the Universities," muttered Cecil to himself. "Now I have no doubt that young ass there, thinks it no end of a fine thing to know those two fellows; either of them would pick his pocket, and one of whom would cut his throat if it suited his purpose. "Well, he looks about good enough for his pals, I will say that for him."

"Poor old Raggles, he is not a bad fellow, rather loud and noisy, perhaps; he doesn't seem to have improved much since he left Cambridge, but he is a good-hearted fellow enough."

"No reason why you should give him a report of your stable, and your chances of winning to-day, to tell to those precious friends of his."

"Well, who are they, that to talk to them is so disgraceful?" queried Jack, looking at the two men to whom Raggles was talking. One of them was of somewhat striking appearance. He stood an inch or two over six feet, but did not look his height; he was both broad-shouldered and deep-chested. He seemed to be well on in middle age, but his black beard and moustache had very little grey in them. He probably would have been good-looking, were it not that his nose had been smashed in, so as to disfigure his face and give it a somewhat sinister expression. He wore a loose suit of blue material, a red handkerchief loosely knotted round his throat, and a brown felt hat. His watch-chain was heavy and looked costly, his fingers were covered with diamonds, suggesting that he understood the advantage of carrying wealth in its most portable shape. There was a brigand-like look about the man, which contrasted with the air of his companion, who had a fresh complexioned face, fat cheeks, small blue eyes and light straw-coloured whiskers. His plump figure was dressed in a black coat, and pepper-and-salt trousers. He looked the essence of sleek respectability.

"Why, the big man calls himself Beamish, *Colonel* Beamish, I daresay; he has as much title to his military rank as he has to his surname. The other is that infernal thief Kit Lukes the lawyer. Beamish professes to be a returned colonist, who has come home with a large fortune. He owns a few horses and bets a good deal, I believe, but the book-makers have not got much of that fortune of his; and it is my opinion that no one would be much the richer for getting the whole of it. Lukes is a sort of racing partner of Beamish. He is a lawyer, who has a lot of shady clients, betting men and low money-lenders, but no one more shady than himself. See, your friend is evidently imparting your information to them, for they are looking at us."

"But every one knows, by this time, that I am confident of winning the Liverpool with the Crier, their knowing it, cannot prevent its winning."

"Don't know so much about that," said Cecil.

The two subjects of Cecil's not very complimentary description, seemed to be as interested in Jack as he was in them.

"Sir John Warleigh, is he? What relation will he be to Captain Warleigh —I don't mean that one yonder—but Warleigh who was in the Lancers, some five and twenty years ago, and was killed in the Crimea?" asked Beamish.

Mr. Lukes replied that the Captain Warleigh he referred to must have been Jack's father, and he went on to explain how Jack came into the baronetcy.

"Well, he is not unlike Jack Warleigh

of the Loyal Lancers either. I should have spotted him for a Warleigh."

"So you knew Sir John's father, did you Colonel? Ah, you would be contemporaries in the army," asked Mr. Lukes, with a curious twinkle in his small blue eyes.

"Yes, we were, and I knew him very well," answered Beamish, without paying much attention, for a second or two, to the insult that was half expressed in the other's tone.

"Let's see, that must have been before you left England, for--where was it you made your fortune?"

"Where one learned not to stand insolence from a shark of a lawyer; and see here, Mr. Lukes, if I want to talk to you about old times, I start in without troubling you to pump me," growled Beamish.

"Well, we have plenty to talk about. I wonder how much there is in what that young fool Raggles told us, about them being so confident of winning at Liverpool with the Crier."

"Looks like it, for I saw Sir John take a thousand to four hundred about it, just now. Yes, he is very like his father, is that youngster, but a bit greener than he was. Any one seems to be welcome to know all he can tell 'em about his horses. It almost makes me wonder whether it mayn't be a plant after all, and he isn't a bit wider awake than every one takes him to be."

"No, he is not that sort; and Captain Warleigh's face showed what he thought of his opening his mouth as he did. By the way—talking of young fools, did you put Raggles on to Jack Sheppard?"

"Yes, he is on fifty, starting price. If he wins, may be it'll come back; and if he loses, it won't hurt us. Ah! there go the numbers."

"Confound 'em, they're backing our horse," said Mr. Lukes, as he heard the book-maker shouting out, all round. "Well, they shall have a run for their money for once; and if they win, they'll back it again for Liverpool. They don't know that we—like Sir John—have a second string to our bow."

"Ay, and one that would win—nineteen years out of twenty," rejoined the Colonel, and then the pair betook themselves to the paddock to say a word or two to the jockey who was to ride their horse, Jack Sheppard.

Jack Sheppard and Clovis were about equal favourites, the public perhaps rather fancying the former. Cecil Warleigh, however, felt extremely confident. His judgment was not often at fault about a horse he had once ridden, and at the last moment, before weighing for the race, he commissioned a book-maker to back his mount for five hundred pounds.

"There goes Clovis with the Captain up, and a right good 'un he is too. If the Crier is so much better than he is, as they say, he will be a thorn in our sides at Liverpool," said Mr. Lukes, when he saw Cecil and Clovis come on to the course.

"There goes Lord Bamborough on Bellman. He has backed his mount as usual, I expect, for they won't lay more than sixes against it. Well, there ain't no accounting for taste; but if I were a lord with twelve thousand a year, I'd set some one else to ride for me, and not risk my noble neck and—there's little Jack!"

Jack Sheppard was a corky-looking little chestnut, that had won as many cross-country races as any horse of his time. Since he had come into the possession of Messrs. Lukes and Beamish he had also lost a good many; when the public had been backing him. His rider was a gentleman who generally had the mount on horses Kit Lukes was interested in, the Honourable Pat Considine, Lord Dargle's brother. The Honourable Pat was as good a rider across country as here and there one. It was a mooted question whether he or Cecil Warleigh was the best; but for all that, Mr. Lukes was one of the few owners who trusted him.

Master Pat never could resist a robbery; and how it was he had never been warned off the turf was a mystery. Certainly it was not because he had family interest; for Lord Dargle, his brother, a sporting nobleman, who was popular and respected, would have been more pleased than any one to see the Honourable Pat banished. Mr. Kit Lukes, however, had an implicit trust in his jockey.

" There's one thing he daren't do ; and that is, to try and humbug me," Kit would say, with a knowing wink. And those who had seen them together, agreed with this.

Jack Warleigh had hurried back to the drag, to watch the race, and had climbed up to sit by the side of Miss Cottingham. Whether he won or lost the race, " this was the best day of his life," he declared to himself.

There were eight starters. Clovis and Jack Sheppard, an Irish horse Danny Mann, the Squire, a horse that had performed very indifferently on the flat, but had shown much promise as a steeplechaser, and four other fairly good horses, who had performed more or less credicably, and might be thought to have some chance of winning. Danny Mann and the Squire were much fancied by their respective stables.

It was a representative field, and three to one was laid at the start against Clovis, who left off half a point better favourite than Jack Sheppard. Danny Mann and the Squire were both six to one.

"Well, to-day ought to tell us what cards we hold in our hands," said Colonel Beamish to the lawyer, as from the top of the Grand Stand he fixed his glasses on the horses at the starting-post.

"Ah, it's a pity that our stable and Sir John Warleigh's should be cutting each other's throats. Wish it was one of the respectable and respected parties I know on the turf who owned 'em," answered Mr. Lukes.

When they were fairly off, Lord Bamborough on the Bellman went to the front and made the running at a tremendous pace. When they passed the Stand, the first time, he was still leading by some lengths, but his horse was nearly pumped out, and shouts of " Any odds against the Bellman," " I'll lay 'gainst the Bellman," greeted his ears as he came past the Ring.

"That's a clever man, mind you, anywhere else. There ain't a leg on the turf could best him. But set him to ride a race, and he's the biggest duffer out," said Kit Lukes to his partner.

"Well, we're going as well as any of 'em. Pat knows what he's about. Clovis is going splendidly, Danny Mann is coming up now," he added, as the Irish horse took up the running from the Bellman, and led the way by half a field. The pace had been hot, and when they were a mile from home, Danny Mann and the two favourites, the former still leading, were the only three in the race.

"Our horse is going well enough, but I think the Captain will win. The Irishman's about done," said Mr. Lukes, who was a wonderfully keen judge of racing, and a thorough sportsman, though a very shady one.

"Ah, the Captain wins! Clovis wins!"

At the next jump, the distance between the Irish horse and his two opponents was diminished considerably, and the Ring seemed to be of Mr. Lukes' opinion, for there were shouts of "sixty to ten against Danny Mann!" "Here. I'll back Clovis! Three hundred to a hundred on Clovis! A thousand to a hundred on Clovis! Any odds on Clovis!" shouted an excited Ringman, as across the last field Cecil Warleigh came away from Jack Sheppard and raced up to the half-beaten Danny Mann. At the last fence the latter led by about half a length, but he was done for, and as he came up to it he half refused. Before he could quite make up his mind to do so, however, the great Irish horseman who rode him set him at it, and he landed on the other side, but as he did so, he swerved across Clovis, and a yell from the Ring told that they were both down.

"We win, partner," said Lukes, as the chestnut took the last fence and came in alone; "but for all that, things look as if these Warleighs have a stronger hand than we have for Liverpool."

CHAPTER XI.

AN AFTER-DINNER NAP.

CECIL was none the worse for his fall, but he had lost a good deal more money than he ought to have done on the race. Nor was he at all better pleased, when he heard his nephew declaring to any one who cared to listen to him, that he was highly satisfied with Clovis' performance, as it proved what the Crier ought to do at Liverpool.

Cecil did not ride again, but on the last two races he managed to double his losses. He also had a word or two with his nephew, which put him out all the more.

"Well, every one knows by this time that Clovis can hardly make the Crier gallop. Don't you think you could find something else to talk about, for a change, instead of running about like a school-boy, and saying the same thing over and over again?" he said interrupting him, as he was discussing his chances of winning the cross country Derby, with a Loamshire County gentleman who was not likely to have more than a fiver on the race.

"After all the horse is mine, and you must allow me to say what I like to my friends," Jack had answered with more heat than he had ever shown before.

"And I have to hold my tongue, do what I'm told, I suppose. You had better get one of your friends to ride for you, for I'll be hanged if I do," he had answered, as he turned away in a passion.

"I am sorry I said anything to annoy you," Jack answered pleasantly, for his irritation was only momentary. "Only no fellow likes being called a fool in so many words, however true it may be."

"Oh, that's all right, I ought not to have been so nasty," Cecil had answered in the same tone. "But losing that race as I did, was enough to put a saint out of temper, and I don't profess to be a saint."

"Confound him, he means to have things his own way," was his inward comment. "Well, it won't do to quarrel with him. What an infernal system the law of entail is, to be sure!"

"Did you hear that?" whispered Beamish to the lawyer. The two happened to be standing very near Cecil, when this conversation took place.

"I guess if the Captain owned the Crier, he might listen to reason. But Sir John is a bit too impetuous and hot-headed. How he reminds me of his father! They never brought me much luck did the Warleighs."

"Wonder what he ever had to do with 'em?" mused Mr. Lukes to himself. "I would like to know what his career has been; perhaps they might tell me at Scotland Yard, only I fancy that broken nose of his has altered him past recognition."

While the Lancers were at Brille-ton, two troops were quartered at Fetchester, and one of these was Cecil Warleigh's. So, when the steeple-chases were over, he had not far to go home. The next day he had some duty to do, or he would have gone back on the drag to head-quarters, and stayed there, for he felt that Fetchester would be depressing, and the reaction that always sets in after a bad day's racing would be specially hard to bear in a dreary little town. For some reasons he was fairly satisfied to be on detachment duty, for he could get more leave, and he found the place convenient for town, but on that special

afternoon he felt thoroughly discontented.
He wished he was out of the army altogether. It was an infernal nuisance, and
he would send in his papers, he declared
to himself, as he left the drag at the
King's Head at Fetchester, and watched
it driven off through the town. There
was a depressing sense of past festivity,
and the place was as flat as a brandy and
soda mixed the night before. The town
had been crammed, but had now emptied
again. The bars and tap-room were
crowded with revellers of the lower
orders, who were making the place
hideous, and getting drunk. All the
better class people had gone. The book-
makers had taken themselves off, and
only the humblest of the camp-followers
of the turf-men, who tramped from race-
course to race-course still remained.
Nor did the barracks afford much hope of
a pleasant evening. Two subalterns
were away on leave, two others, so he
happened to remember, were dining out.
He was destined to a *tête-a-tête* dinner
with McGloom, the other Captain.
Now no human being would ever call
McGloom a choice spirit. Like Quilp, he
could not have been one had he wished to
be ; and, as a matter of fact he did not
wish. He had lately surprised, and to a

certain extent alarmed his brother officers,
by taking a serious turn, and had adopted
the principles of the Elected Brethren,
because, as far as he understood them,
they gave him the best grounds for form-
ing the worst possible opinion as to the
present state and future destiny of the
largest section of his fellow-men.   There
was only one secular subject which the
great change in his life had not put on
one side.   That was a recollection of a
certain steeple-chase he had attended,
some half dozen years since, when Cecil
had very unwisely advised him to back
his mount ; and McGloom, believing that
Cecil knew something, had followed his
advice to the extent of backing him for
three sovereigns.   The horror of the
moment when he discovered that Cecil
was not going to win, and that he was
fated to have to pay three sovereigns,
was still fresh in his memory.   Cecil,
since he had been on detachment, had
often wished that he had paid the money
for him, there and then.   It was useless
for Cecil to urge, that when a man
advised a friend to back a horse, that
was at six to one, he could hardly be
regarded in the light of an insurer.

"Ah call it varra bad form, to get
your friend to throw away his money in

backing a horse that had no airthly chance,"
he would say, after he had told, again and
again, the monotonous story of that race—
the last he ever witnessed—for his loss gave
him a distaste for that branch of sport.

"Ah'm afraid there's a gude deal of
dishonesty and roguery mixed up in it all,"
he would add—by way of comment.
Though if directly tackled by Cecil, as to
what he meant by this remark he would
take care to deny having any intention to
give personal application to it. The fact
of the steeple-chase having occurred, would
be certain to give him an opportunity for
harking back to his pet grievance.

Cecil had asked Jack to stay and dine with
him, but Jack, on hearing that Kate Cottingham was going on, after the steeple-
chases, to a watering-place some thirty
miles off, and would go to a ball in the
evening, had determined to go thither
also; a proceeding which made Cecil feel
particularly annoyed with Jack, and thoroughly alive to the intense folly and
weakness of his character.

"How different everything would be if
Jack were only out of the way," he found
himself thinking. After he had added up
the amount he had lost, he had come to
the conclusion, that he would find it very
difficult to settle. Altogether, he felt

there was nothing to do in the town
to help him ward off a fit of the blues;
and he would give anything for some sort
of excitement. It was a fitting ending to
a wretchedly unlucky day, this being left
in such a hole of a place with no chance
of getting his money back again.

As he glanced through the door of the
King's Head, the principal hotel at Fetchester, the idea of a "Sherry-and-bitters,"
suggested itself to him, and he went in, and
talked over the events of the day with Miss
Cutts, who presided in the bar-parlour.

" Well, I am sorry you didn't win, Captain, I had my money on you, and so had
Charles, and the boots. Though the party
who owns Jack Sheppard—Colonel Beamish he is called, I think—is staying in
the house, and is very pleasant and affable—told us all to back his horse. By the
way, Charles, when does number two go
up to town ? "

" Doesn't go up till to-morrow. He'll
dine here with Mr. Raggles this evening,"
answered the waiter.

" To be sure he does. I daresay you
know Mr. Raggles, Captain, son of Mr.
Raggles, of Brown and Raggles, the
manufacturers."

Captain Warleigh said that he hadn't
that honour, and was about to leave, when

Beamish and a young man, whom Cecil recognized as Jack's old college friend, and whom he rightly put down to be Mr. Raggles, came into the bar-parlour.

The latter, although there were already signs about him that he had not confined himself to non-intoxicants, ordered a " gin and bitters."

" Well, Captain Warleigh, you had bitter bad luck to-day," said Colonel Beamish, who had a slight acquaintance with Cecil. " It looked any odds on you when Tom O'Brien upset you. Hope you got it back on the other races ? "

Cecil's only answer was a shake of the head, which Beamish rightly interpreted as a negative.

" There were one or two good things I could have told you of. That Hunter's Stakes, nice useful price, the winner started at two."

" Yes, we knocked the bookies this round," said Mr. Raggles, addressing himself to Warleigh—whom he did not know —with the easy freedom of partial intoxication. " I had 'em for six hundred."

Cecil, as he looked at Colonel Beamish, thought to himself that he knew where most of the six hundred would find its way. It annoyed him rather, to think that a young greenhorn like Raggles should win when he had lost.

"Are you staying in this lively city? I am dining with this sportsman. Do you know him? Mr. Raggles—Captain Warleigh," said Beamish, who rather doubted whether Warleigh would not resent the impertinence of his introducing a friend, but determined to do it; as he knew it would please Mr Raggles.

"Know your nephew Jack very well. He tells me that he's going to have it all his own way at Liverpool—but I don't know that he hasn't made another mistake. He thought it was a certainty to-day, you know."

"I am quartered here for my sins," said Cecil, in answer to Beamish's question, without paying much attention to Mr. Raggles' remarks, which reminded him of his grievance against Jack.

"Look here, Captain Warleigh—why not join us at dinner? When I dine here Hickman manages to send up a fairish dinner, and some decentish booze. It ain't over-rollicking up at the barracks, I should say," broke in Mr. Raggles.

Cecil Warleigh did not much care about improving Raggles' acquaintance, nor did he consider that Colonel Beamish was a man with whom it was very desirable to become very intimate. On the other hand, anything almost seemed better than a dreary dinner at the barracks. In fact he had been half thinking of dining at the hotel by himself. Beamish undoubtedly was sometimes very well informed about racing matters, and an evening spent in his society might not altogether be unprofitable. So after a little hesitation he accepted the invitation. So far as Colonel Beamish's behaviour went, Cecil had no reason to regret having consented to dine with him. The Colonel made himself agreeable, and had plenty to say about racing. He discussed the events of the forthcoming season in a way that was well worth attention, and on the other hand showed no wish to pump him in return. Mr. Raggles, who, though he ate very little, paid great attention to the drinkables, got unpleasantly familiar, as he became unpleasantly intoxicated. In this condition he did not improve on acquaintance.

"Tell you what, old chap. I can't understand you being such a flat as to drop your money to-day. Any one who knew anything at all about it, must have made a bit," said Raggles in a tone of familiarity, which had a peculiarly irritating effect on Cecil, and he went on exulting over his winnings, continually harking back to the subject.

Beamish winked at Cecil, and pointed to his glass.

" He wouldn't have got much, Captain, unless I had been at his elbow. Wish I had had an opportunity of telling you about the Hunter's Stakes. My opinion is that there ought to be more give and take between owners."

Cecil did not say much in reply, he was inclined to think Beamish was a little too civil.

" Well, suppose we have a gamble ? Aye, you're longing to have the fingering of some of my winnings, ain't you, Warleigh ? Like to have a little bit to settle with, on Monday ? And that old shark there ?" said Raggles, pointing to Beamish : " he is always game to gamble, as I know to my cost."

To tell the truth, Mr. Raggles was not far wrong as to Cecil's feelings. He had been longing for some way of gambling ever since he had left the race-course. To a certain extent that feeling had influenced him in accepting the invitation to dinner. However, when Mr. Raggles suggested cards, he had considerable misgivings. First of all he felt doubtful of the wisdom of encountering that some-

what mysterious warrior, Colonel Beamish. Then it was pretty obvious that
Mr. Raggles was not quite in a fit state to
play. His first ground for misgivings was
removed by the Colonel announcing that
he felt inclined to take a nap, and was too
sleepy. "Besides there are too many or
too few. You and the Captain have a
game at *ecarté*, and I'll take it easy,"
Beamish said, lighting a cigar and throwing himself on a sofa.

Warleigh was irresolute. Certainly he
would like to settle the rather awkward
question of "ways and means" at the
expense of Mr. Raggles. To settle his
accounts on the following Monday would
require a loan from Jack, who had lately
shown that he was beginning to realize
that the spending capacities of his fortune
were not boundless. Cecil disliked the
idea of going to him for help just then
particularly, as for reasons of his
own he felt anything but well dis-
posed to him, and was inclined to feel
more keenly than ever he did, that his
young kinsman was very much in the
way.

But then to play with Raggles, who
was momentarily getting more and more
tipsy, was not very reputable. Still it
was not his business to see that Raggles

was not sober, and after all he had not
proposed cards. Far from it, Raggles
was worrying him to play.

"Don't feel very inclined for it, still I
should not mind playing *ecarté* for an
hour or so," he said at last.

Beamish's cigar had dropped from his
mouth and he was snoring, so the two
were practically alone.

"Right you are, *ecarté* is my game.
Look here, we'll play ten games, twenty-
five pounds a game," said Raggles, and
taking up a pack, he began to sort out
the small cards. The way he performed
this, bore witness to his condition. It
is impossible to say how long he would
have been over the cards, if Cecil had
not undertaken it for him.

"Well, we'll play as you like," said
Cecil as he cut for deal.

No, it was no business of his to notice
that the youngster was drunk, and after
all, how was he to know that it was
not his ordinary manner? But, as they
played, Cecil's inconvenient scruples began
to rise again. Now Raggles would
expose his hand by mistake,—then he
forgot to mark the king. But to drunken
men there is an exception to the rule
that cards never forgive. Fortune made
up for all Raggles' blunders. Though he

forgot to mark the king, he made a trick with it, and the court cards of trumps seemed never to be out. By sheer bad play he lost several games, but Cecil had wretched cards as a rule, and at the end of the first ten games Raggles was fifty pounds to the good. Raggles proposed ten more games for fifty. Cecil agreed to it, he had become savage and determined to win; his scruples did not trouble him any longer. They each won five games. Beamish still snored in peace as they played.

"*Ecarté* is all infernal rot, too slow a game," said Raggles. "Let's change it to something more lively: say poker, let'sh play poker."

"Single poker is rather a cut-throat sort of game, isn't it?" queried Cecil, as he coolly took stock of his young friend who was every minute getting more incapable.

"You're not afraid, are you? Have a limit if you don't care to play too high; but if we go on playing at this rot we shall play without either of us being better or worse for it."

"I think a limit is nonsense, but just as you like," answered Cecil, who knew perfectly well that poker, particularly single poker, is just the game at which a drunken man is most likely to come to serious grief. Cecil, however, had sworn to himself that one of them should be decidedly the better before it was over.

"I don't mind playing poker, but I won't go on long," he said, taking up the cards and shuffling them.

"Shall we wake up old Beamish, there, and have three?" said Raggles, pointing to the recumbent figure of the colonel.

"We shall do very well as we are," Cecil said as he put the cards down.

Raggles gulped down a brandy and soda, and then after a few words about the amount of the blind—Cecil wasted no time in making a demur about the play being too high—the game began.

The two were ill-matched enough. Raggles tipsy and excited; Cecil cool, and determined to make the most of every chance. The knowledge that he was doing a rather shady thing, which to a certain extent oppressed him, only seemed to steady his nerves, and make him greedy to win. But fortune still kept faithful to Raggles, and the worse his cards were, the more reckless his play became. The drink he had taken told more and more upon him, but still his good luck made up for his bad play. He was a hundred pounds to the good at poker, and Cecil was beginning to feel very savage with him. After one draw Raggles stupidly exposed his hand. Cecil was beginning to tell him what he had done, when he doubled. Cecil had seen that he had three aces, a four and a six in his hand. He himself held a full hand of kings, high. Cecil tried to argue with himself that after all, he only had a glimpse of the cards, and could not be quite sure that Raggles had not two fours, but notwith-withstanding, he doubled in return. Raggles with the obstinacy of a drunken man, doubled again. Cecil again doubled; and so they went on until the stake became nine hundred pounds. Then Raggles made it eighteen hundred. "That ought to be about enough to win him," thought Cecil.

"I will see your cards. Full hand. Kings high," cried Cecil.

"Full hand. Aces high," said Raggles, "no, stay! three aces, a four, and a six! confounded mistake," corrected Raggles.

"Eighteen hundred to me," said Cecil, calmly pushing a pencil and some paper across the table.

Raggles scrawled an I.O.U. for the amount. "I'll have a drink after that," he said, and getting up, he lurched across the room, and pulled at the bell. The rope coming off in his hands, he came down in a heap in the corner of the room. Almost at the same moment, the waiter, who had probably been in the passage, entered, in answer to the summons, and Beamish seemed to wake up at the same moment.

CHAPTER XII.

COLONEL BEAMISH WIDE AWAKE.

"Gad! how I've slept! Hallo! our noisy young friend had better be got to bed. Help Mr. Raggles to No. 3, waiter. Take something before you go, Captain Warleigh," said the colonel.

Cecil was carefully folding up Raggles' I.O.U., and about to put it into his betting-book.

"Thank you, but I've already done very well," then after a word or two of farewell, he took his departure. His winnings amounted to about sixteen hundred pounds. "It will come in very useful," Cecil thought, as he walked back to the barracks; but he couldn't help wishing that Mr. Raggles had kept himself a little bit straighter, and not have made such an utter collapse at the finish. It did not look well. Then the matter of the last nine hundred pounds that he had won came back very unpleasantly to his conscience. He had never done anything quite like that before. It was just as if he had taken the money from him, for he had known all the time he was raising the bets, that Raggles had a worse hand than his. Well, it would have been much the same if he had not known for certain, for he would have guessed that Raggles was bluffing, he tried to persuade himself, but it was not much good. It was not his business to look after Raggles. He did not propose the game; and the money he had won would come in very opportunely. He wondered whether Raggles would pay up, or want time. Hang it, he ought to pay up at once; and this thought suggested a train of thoughts, in which he forgot the twinges of conscience which had troubled him; and, turning into bed, he slept the sleep of the just.

Next morning, waking refreshed from his sleep, Cecil was inclined to take rather a favourable view of his last night's proceedings. He quite persuaded himself, that he had not really seen Raggles' cards in that hurried glance he got at them.

The young cad stunk of money, and the sixteen hundred pounds would come in very useful. As for Raggles being drunk, he was not going to admit any such thing, his legs may have been wrong, but his head was right enough. Had he not won all the evening, until just the last *coup?* Anyhow, it would be a good bit pleasanter than having to go to Jack for the money. It was perhaps a lucky thing for him, he began to think, that Beamish went to sleep in the way he did. Something suggested to him, that if·the Colonel had taken a hand, his luck perhaps would not have been quite so good as it was. He was in a drowsy state, looking at his bath, and thinking that he must get up soon, when he heard a voice in the passage inquiring for him, and then there was a knock at his door, and in walked the very gentleman he had been thinking so complacently about, viz. Colonel Beamish.

"Excuse me, Captain, for taking you so early," began the Colonel, as he took up a position in front of the fire, "but I am off by the eleven train, and thought that maybe I shouldn't catch you, unless I dropped in first thing."

Cecil took advantage of his position as a man in bed, and therefore not obliged to be energetic in entertaining his visitor. What he wondered at was 'why had the Colonel taken the trouble to call on him at all?'

"Well, I daresay you can guess what I've come about," remarked Beamish, "it's about last night's business."

"Don't remember that we had any business together, Colonel Beamish," said Cecil, beginning to feel rather uncomfortable.

"I take it, so far as I could make out, and I followed the game pretty closely, that you had that youngster last night for about sixteen or seventeen hundred pounds."

"You allow yourself to use rather remarkable language, Colonel Beamish ; but if you mean how much did I win at cards, you are not far out in your estimate."

"I mean pretty much what I said," answered Beamish, with provoking coolness, "but it will be time enough to argue when we understand each other."

"Well, I suppose you've come from Mr. Raggles?" asked Cecil.

"Mr. Raggles is sleeping off last night's drink. No, I come on my own account. I have a little proposition to make about that money. It is simple enough. I say 'halves' in the plunder."

"What the devil do you mean?" shouted Cecil, sitting up in bed, now thoroughly awake. "It may be customary among your friends and confederates, that the gang should share in any money that any of their number win at play, but

I've not the honour of belonging to that section of society."

" Yet, when you play with a boy who is blind drunk, and win nine hundred pounds from him on a deal at poker, after you looked over his hand, you show that you would not be so very strange in that section of society, if ever it was your lot to join it."

" Leave my quarters, or I'll kick you out of them," said Cecil, jumping out of bed, and approaching his visitor in a threatening manner.

" Go slow, and keep your hands off me," said Colonel Beamish. " You have more than twenty-five years the best of me, but you wouldn't find it an easy job, however, try it, if you like ; but while you are putting your boots on to kick me out, listen to me. I was not asleep last night. Now just ask yourself the question, Am I the sort of man who would be likely to go to sleep while heavy play was going on ? "

Cecil clenched his teeth. Looking back it seemed to him, for a customer like Colonel Beamish to have slept quietly through the rather curious transactions of the evening before was a very unlikely proceeding. Besides he seemed to have a very clear notion of what had taken place. Cecil remembered, however, the sort of character he had to deal with, and determined to put a bold face on the matter.

"Last night, after having been repeatedly asked to do so by Mr. Raggles, I consented to play cards. That he was not sober when he played, whatever he may have been afterwards, I utterly deny. As for your other statement, all I have to say is, that it is an impudent falsehood, thoroughly in keeping with your brazen attempt to extort money. If Mr. Raggles ever wishes to mix in more respectable society than yours, he had better pay his losses. As for you, I shall take the opinion of a criminal lawyer."

"Not bad, Captain, but you haven't seen my hand as clearly as you did Raggles last night. You see I have a card or two you have not reckoned up. It's not only my word against yours. See here how it is. When that young ass wakes up and remembers something about last night, he'll ask me what happened. I tell him he was drunk and was robbed when he was drunk. It won't be only my evidence, but his. Then there will be the waiter who cleared away dinner, at half-past nine, and will have to say that he was pretty well three parts drunk then, and that at one, when he took him to bed, he was blind and speechless. Between half-past nine and one, you won seventeen hundred pounds off him. Rather an ugly story that."

Cecil Warleigh realized that it would be a very ugly story. He wished to goodness he had kept clear of Beamish and Raggles.

"Well, Captain," Beamish went on, "if I take that line I shall improve my position with that young ass Raggles, and a good bit of that seventeen hundred pounds will find its way here," and the Colonel slapped his pocket. "But see here ; suppose I say to him that though he got a bit 'cut' afterwards, he was as steady as a rock while the play went on, and that there is no earthly excuse for his not paying. Why then he will find the money. He can do it easily enough, mind you, and when it is divided up, there will be eight hundred odd apiece, and may be, I can show you how to make that eight hundred into a good deal more. When I saw you winning that fool's money, I thought to myself that you and I were partners for the night, and what a pity it was, so I thought, that we weren't going to be partners in one or two other little things. Believe me, Captain, I could show you how to bring a rare good week off, before many days are over, if you and I were pals."

"You have a queer way of putting things," said Cecil gloomily. He certainly did not like the look of the turn affairs had taken. He would, he thought, be glad enough to give up the money he had won, but if he did, there would be an ugly story against him, which would most likely sooner or later get wind. After all, it seemed safer to keep on good terms with Beamish.

"Now, don't mistake me, I don't want to dine with you at mess, or to slap you on the back, or to parade the fact that we are pals. We shouldn't do each other much good by my doing that; but on the quiet, don't you think that we might, now and then, play into each other's hands. Now, to show that I mean business. I'll tell you what. You need not give me more than six hundred of that money. I must have that, for it ain't likely I let the young fool win money yesterday, at the races, without intending to get hold of his winnings."

Warleigh looked uncomfortable, but he had ceased to be indignant. Yes, looking carefully at the matter, he thought that the best thing he could do, was to shut Beamish's mouth, and let him settle matters quietly. As for any future dealings with Beamish, he promised himself that he would have as little as possible to do with that very dangerous gentleman.

"Well, you can have the money," he said rather suddenly.

"That's sensible, just write out a memo. to that effect, not that it is wanted perhaps, only if after I have persuaded young Raggles to send you a cheque—as he will do, mind you, before many hours are over—you somehow forget this little arrangement, why I should have a card to play. No, just write a promise to pay me six hundred pounds on receiving a cheque from Raggles," and Beamish looked round the room, and finding some writing materials, brought them to the table by the bed. "No, don't take it amiss. It's the first time we have done business, and one likes to have everything straight. After a bit, no doubt you and I will be on more confidential terms, and shall become as thick as thieves."

Cecil Warleigh, thought the last expression a singularly ill-chosen one, but for all that he wrote what the other wanted. As he did so, Beamish took out a sporting paper from his pocket.

"They have sent the Crier to fours for the Grand National. Absurd price! you say. Well, that is just what it is. It ain't the certainty that some people think either. I know an outsider at thirties, which is well worth backing. In fact, in any other year—with the Crier out of the way, I know how that thousand pounds you will take off young Raggles might be made into a niceish bit."

"But the Crier won't be out of the way, he will start, and I think he'll win. But fours to one is an absurd price."

"You don't think there is any chance of Sir John being got to see reason?" asked Beamish, looking into Cecil's face, as if he were trying to read his thoughts.

"Not the slightest," Cecil answered.

"Well, it can't be helped. It's a pity too that two parties should cut each other's throats; this ain't a world to lose good chances in; just for the want of a little arrangement. See here, Captain, you'll be up in town next week, drop me a line to Tankard's Hotel, and we'll meet somewhere quietly, and have a little talk, until then, take my tip, and don't be in a hurry to take fours about the Crier. Good morning!" and the Colonel swaggered out of the room.

The less he saw of that dubious warrior the better, Cecil Warleigh's better self told him ; yet a few moments afterwards he was thinking that he might just as well learn something about the outsider the Colonel spoke about.

CHAPTER XIII.

WINDMILL LODGE.

JACK WARLEIGH had agreed to drive Cecil over to Windmill Lodge, where Tom Ring's stables were, the day after the Fetchester Steeple-chases. In old Sir George's time, three or four rooms at the Lodge had been furnished very comfortably, and he had spent a good deal of time there, looking after his horses, coming and going when he liked, and being perfectly free from the restraint and observation to which he was subjected at Warleigh Hall. The hounds were meeting on the following day, very near the Lodge ; so it was arranged that Cecil should stay a day or two there, to confer with Tom Ring, ride the Crier in his gallops, and run his eye over some of the other horses in training.

Jack was by no means one of those unhappy-tempered men, who after a slight difference with any one, are never—as they like to put it—quite the same again. He considered that Cecil had spoken very nicely afterwards. He thought of their dispute, however, when he found—as he did—that he had to break his engagement.

"I'm awfully sorry, old chap," he said, as he bustled into the ante-room at the barracks, about the time he had arranged to call for Cecil, "but I can't go to Windmill Lodge this afternoon. There is a political meeting here, that I ought to attend. You see, one ought to go in for those sort of things. Life isn't all beer and skittles, one has one's duties, and all that. It is an infernal bore, but one has got to go in for it. You see, old Sir George and the late baronet were prominent politicians, and I must take my part, too. There's the dog-cart for you to drive over in, and I shall be there to-morrow evening. I hope you won't mind."

"No, I shall be all right by myself," Cecil said; and he spoke the truth. His nephew's society rather bored him than otherwise just then. "And you are quite right to go in for those sort of things. You ought to be member for the county, and will be, next General Election. You'll make a deuced sight better member than poor George was. He was everlastingly running about the country and delivering speeches—a hash of newspaper articles—to a bored village audience. I don't believe any one ever listened to one of them without pondering over the advantages of definitely going over to the other side, and so never by any chance having to listen to him again."

"I am glad you think I am doing the right thing, and to tell you the truth I have some idea of doing what you mention."

"Cromwell! I charge thee, fling away ambition," quoted Cecil laughingly; "but seriously I think you are right. You don't know what it is to come to my age, and feel that you have never done anything more than ride and shoot; but you have a better chance than I ever had."

As he said this Cecil's manner was pleasant enough, but for all that, he recognized the sermon that had produced this effect upon his nephew, and the train of thought that was suggested thereby was not over-pleasing.

"Lord Whippenham comes down this afternoon and some of us are to meet him, and there is a dinner to-night and a meeting to-morrow, so there will be no hunting for me. I hope they'll make you comfortable at the lodge."

"You bet they will. It won't be the first time I've stayed there, by a good many. Well, good luck to you. Make a good speech at the dinner," he added as Jack hurried away to his political duties.

"Dashed young ass ; he seems to feel himself a Cabinet Minister at least, because he is taking part in a twopenny-halfpenny meeting," Cecil said to himself as he prepared to start for Windmill Lodge.

The trainer's house and stables stood on the edge of a long stretch of undulating heath land. Behind it were some acres of plantation, round the tan gallop. Everything about the place was perfect, for it was built by old Sir George, who, hardly pressed for money or not, never knew what it was to stint expense in his amusements. The place stood quiet enough, for it was just five miles from any village, but a private wire from the house put it in communication with the rest of the world.

"Glad to see you, Captain ; but where is Sir John ?" asked Tom Ring, a handsome, fresh-looking man, who came out of the house as the dog-cart was driven into the yard.

"He thinks he is bound to go and support Lord Whippenham, at the dinner to-night, and the meeting to-morrow, Ring," said Cecil.

"I am glad of it, Captain, he ought to be there. I'd like to be there myself, and say what I think about things," said the trainer, who in a way was a well-read man, and took great interest in politics, being fond of the sound of his own voice. "The lodge looks well, doesn't it? Everything is trim and smart again, and the stables are worthy of the horses that are in 'em?" he continued, looking complacently round at the buildings and outhouses; no doubt thanking his stars that a baronet fond of sport once again ruled at Warleigh.

"It was a bad business, that at Fetchester, wasn't it, Captain? You were winning easy enough though; but it shows up our form as being pretty good, doesn't it?"

Cecil Warleigh was the one man whom Tom Ring admired from the bottom of his heart. When he was a boy about the stables, in his father's time, Cecil had just joined the service, and was his ideal gentleman. Cecil won the first Grand National he had ever seen. Cecil was one of the few whom he would admit to be his superior as a horseman, and he was inclined to allow that he knew almost as much about his own business of training as he did himself. Cecil could do, well, all the things he best understood; so he made a hero of him, and thought he could do anything he liked.

Five years before, an incident had happened which had greatly added to Cecil's influence over Tom Ring. The latter's only child, a little girl, then but five years old, to whom he was devoted, had been playing near the weir on the Loam, which runs half-a-mile from Windmill Lodge. Cecil had been staying there with his father, and was whiling away the afternoon by spinning for pike in the mill dam. Tom Ring was some way off fishing, and the little girl had strayed down after him, but he had not noticed her, and no one was looking after her. Cecil had hooked a pike and was just landing it when he heard a child's scream. Looking round, he saw the flaxen-haired little girl topple from the woodwork of the sluice, on which she had climbed, right into the pool below the lasher. Tom Ring saw Cecil drop his rod, hurry to the side of the weir, and plunge into the stream. He hurried to where he saw the splash, and came in time to see Cecil struggling to the bank, with the little girl in his arms. There was, perhaps, no very great danger in

what Cecil had done, though there was a
treacherous under-current at the spot, but
Tom Ring never forgot it. He would do
anything for the Captain—anything that
one man could ask of another. To have
a chance of showing how grateful he was
would be his greatest pleasure.

After Cecil had eaten a capital dinner
and sat smoking a cigar and finishing
a bottle of old port, which had been
some of a stock laid down at the lodge
in old Sir George's time, the wine was
too good to be smoked over—but Cecil
found a cigar irresistible,—Tom Ring
came into the room. It was the sitting-
room furnished twenty years before by
old Sir George, and its walls, if they
could speak, could have told some strange
tales of high play between the old baronet
and his racing cronies, and of various
other matters.

After accepting a cigar, Tom Ring
drew a stiff-backed chair to the table,
and helped himself to a glass of wine,
Cecil leaning back in a roomy arm-chair,
in which he remembered so well seeing
his father sit.

" Well, Tom, what about Liverpool and
the Crier ? They appear to think it is as
good as over, by the betting. Did ever
man hear of such an absurd price ? "

" Well, Captain, three to one is a short price for a cross-country race. But I don't know. He's bound to win, I think. He's one of the old sort. There ain't any like him nowadays. He's a Triton among minnows."

" Three to one is too short a price to take ; at least for a man of my means, Tom."

" You see there ain't anything else in the race according to my notions. Nothing of the same class," answered the trainer. " Lord Bamborough's horse ain't near the Crier, and if he were, his lordship can't ride a race ; and they say he means riding himself."

" Yes, he means riding, and I'm not afraid of him, but there's no telling what there mayn't be against one," answered Cecil, and he began to think of Colonel Beamish and his outsider.

" We have some other pretty smartish ones in at Sandham, and we ought to pick up a race or two there. I don't know what is wrong with Sir Roland, but there's no getting him right again. Gallop him a quarter-of-a-mile and he's certain to pull up dead lame. It's a pity too, for he is a good-looking horse, ain't unlike the Crier; only he ain't worth a farthing," said Tom Ring, and then he began to discuss other animals in his stables.

"Please, Mr. Ring," said a maid-servant who was clearing away the cloth, "there is Joe Lees—gipsy Joe as they call him—wants to see you, and when I said you was up here talking with the Captain, he said 'the Captain might as well hear what he had to say to you.'"

"I remember the rascal, he used always to be lurking about the woods, when the horses were being galloped," said Cecil.

"Yes, a rank tout, but Sir John doesn't mind the public knowing what his horses do; in fact, he seems to like it," answered Ring.

Joe Lees was a long, dark-skinned fellow—with a not unpleasant expression in his bold dark eyes. He had been, in his time, a good deal at war with the powers that be, but for all that, he could be quite at his ease with the respectable part of the community whenever he met them.

"Hope I see you well, Captain? None the worse for that fall in the big race? I were main sorry to see you beat by a mean bloke like that Pat Considine. I owe him one for pulling a horse, and losing me three crowns. I nearly paid him out at Worcester last year, afore the races. I were asleep along side of the course, under a hedge, when this 'ere 'honourable' as they calls him, comes a-walking round the course, 'aving a squint at the jumps. When I twigged him and sees no one nigh, I gets in front of him and says, 'bain't you the Honourable Pat Considine?'"

"'Yes, I am,' he says quite affable, 'but I don't know you.'

"'No, but you blam'd soon will, for I'm going to give you the best 'idin' you ever had. You pulled a horse last spring and lost me three crowns. Will you fight?'

"'No, gipsy,' he says, 'I can't fight, but I can run like blazes,' and off he starts before I can get at him, and never stops running till he gets to the Grand Stand, bless yer, he didn't wait to deny having pulled the horse."

Cecil laughed merrily at the notion of Pat Considine's discomfiture. "If he had a thrashing for every race he's pulled, he wouldn't have a sound bone in his body," he said.

"Well, Joe, and what is your business?" asked Tom Ring, who was anxious to know what the gipsy had come about.

"Well, it's a little bit of news I wished

to give you, gov'ner. There's a cove come down from London to watch our horses, and he'll be on the ground to-morrow."

"Ah, Mr. Joe, you don't like any one to peach on your preserves, do you?" said Tom Ring with a laugh.

"No, I don't want strangers from London humbugging about, not that I believe he is one who could see what was going on, if he was on the ground. I s'pose he'd heard that I knew summut about horses, for he comes and gives me a bob, and axes me to come out with him to-morrow, saying, ' he warn't quite sure about the horses and didn't feel certain he knew which was which, as it wer' a long time since he see the Crier.' "

"Well, Joe, here's another bob for you," said Tom Ring, "but the party from London may come and welcome to see anything there is to be seen. We aren't so strict about touting as we used to be in old Sir George's time."

"That's a main pity, it makes information worth so little," said gipsy Joe, grinning. In those old days he had generally managed to learn all he wanted to know.

"Take a glass," said Cecil, passing a decanter of whiskey towards him, "and drink to your next merry meeting with Pat Considine."

The gipsy helped himself pretty stiffly to whiskey, and after he had put the glass down he winked at Mr. Ring, and said : " It was a pity that the party from London should go back without having learned something worth knowing."

Cecil seemed to coincide with this notion.

" I take it, Joe, if there was anything to be seen, you'd take care he didn't miss it, supposing we got up something for him to see."

" That's it, Captain ! you're fly ; that's just what I thought on. A cove that comes from London to see our horses ought to learn some'at for his pains."

" Now, mind you, Joe. I'll ride the Crier to-morrow ; Mr. Ring will be on Clovis," said Cecil, " and here is another five shillings for you, and now you may take another glass of whiskey, and mind to-morrow morning that the party from London doesn't miss anything."

" What were you telling me about Sir Roland ? " Cecil asked of Ring, after the gipsy had taken his departure. " Goes lame after he has been galloped a bit, you say ? And he has something of the Crier's appearance ? "

" It would serve him thundering well right if we were to play a trick like that on him and those who employ him. But do you think Sir John would like it?" asked the trainer. " For my part, I hate the lot who come sniffing about training quarters, trying to pick up any bit of information."

" Oh, depend upon it," replied Cecil, " he would see the fun of the thing. It would be a rare joke, and teach them not to send men bothering down here, where they're not wanted. Gipsy Joe would take care that the fellow would take it in right enough."

It would be a very good joke for Sir John and for himself too, Cecil thought, as he pondered the circumstance over in his mind. He did not altogether look at the matter in a humorous light. The effect of giving the tout something to telegraph back to London might be to have a very bracing effect on the book-makers, and induce them to lay a reasonable price against the Crier.

CHAPTER XIV.

A VERY PRACTICAL JOKE.

A LITTLE before day-break, the party from London stumbled through the main street of Broughton, a large straggling village some four miles from Tom Ring's stables to the village green, where gipsy Joe had appointed to meet him.

"Well, gov'nor, do you find it airy enough?" said that worthy with a grin as he noticed the other's face, which looked blue with cold.

"Hawful! hawful! 'ang the country and genuine information. Give me a nice warm public-house parlour, and a 'go' of hot gin and water afore me, a jockey boy a-drinking champagne and a-smoking cigars, and a-talking about what goes on in his stables, and I don't mind getting hinformation that way, but as for going out of a mornin' to see 'orses do their gallops, it ain't nowise good enough for Jimmy Bulbeck, who can do better than get in ‘the know’ that way, any day. But there, bless yer, Mr. Raggles he will have it. ‘Bulbeck,’ he says, ‘I should like you to have a look at Tom Ring’s lot. Captain Warleigh is a-goin’ over there, and maybe there’ll be some’at to see.’ I ’ate the job, I do. Warn’t it at Tom Ring’s that a lout got arf eat by a dawg, a year ago?”

“No, that were at Bill Holmes’ in the next county, but it were Tom Ring’s stables the party went to as never were ’eard of agin. He ’adn’t many near friends, I suppose, an’ when he didn’t come back agin, nobody missed him.

“He larnt somethin’ that bloke did, as old Abel Ring, for it was in the old ’uns time, didn’t want to go no further. Nobody missed him, but if they come to me and give me blunt enough to make me blab, I’d show ’em where he lies six foot under ground,” and the gipsy laughed grimly.

“’Anged if I go humbuggin’ out there at all,” said Mr. Bulbeck, looking back in the direction of the inn, where he had slept. There ain’t likely to be what one would call a trial, an’ I don’t want to see it if there is,” he added with a shudder.

“Don’t be afeared, gov’ner! You’re all right with me, you come along, and mind yer, I doan’t say but what we may see some'at like a trial," said the gipsy, and he set out to walk at a brisk rate, Mr. Bulbeck shambling along after him, grumbling to himself anent the dangers and difficulties of the service on which he was engaged. Bulbeck still had the countenance and support of Mr. Raggles, for though the latter gentleman had aspired to become more of a sporting character than he had been when an undergraduate, even to the extent of being in with such very sharp customers as Colonel Beamish and Mr. Kit Lukes, he still was faithful to his old idol, Mr. Jimmy Bulbeck. It had happened that the latter by some piece of luck had advised him to back the winner of the Cambridgeshire, that started at forty to one. And though it was the only one of about eight certainties that he had persuaded his patron to back, still the circumstance was enough to confirm Mr. Raggles' faith, and he continued to send Mr. Bulbeck about to watch trials and report to him of horses. The reports, so far, had not been of any great value, but they satisfied Mr. Raggles, who, however, had become a little more wide awake than he used to be, so that Bulbeck found it to his advantage to visit the places where the horses upon which he had to report were trained. On one occasion he had really been present at an important trial, and he was paid well for his information, not only by Mr. Raggles, but by two or three book-makers to whom he retailed what he had learned.

"They will be on the tan, for there's a good bit of frost in the ground," said gipsy Joe, after they had done four miles and had come in sight of the house. Bulbeck assented to this remark with a cold shiver.

It was a nasty lonely place, he thought, and then the gipsy's grim story of the missing man whose body could be found six feet under ground, came back unpleasantly to his mind.

"I'd as soon a'most take to welching again as go on with this game, it's hugly work that's what it is," he said to himself as he scrambled through a gap in a fence and followed the gipsy along a narrow path.

"Look out where you walk ! There was a cove killed in a man-trap just about here, three years ago," said the gipsy, who took a malicious pleasure in watching Bulbeck's nervous alarm aroused by his anecdotes. They had some little time to wait after they had hidden themselves in some bushes, so gipsy Joe improved the occasion by inventing a blood-hound and fearfully maligning Tom Ring, whom he described as a "reg'lar chip of the old block," and who he said would be a deal crueller than old Abel Ring in a year or two, "gets more and more like the old chap in his ways every hour he do."

At length in the quiet of the keen frosty morning air, they could hear voices at the stables, and soon a string of eight horses in clothing came through the gateway into the plantation.

"There's the Captain. He's a cool 'un he is. If he on'y knows we was 'ere," said the gipsy, who was watching with a good deal of interest to see what was going to be done, what farce had been got up for Bulbeck's benefit.

"Tom Ring's going to ride Clovis, the 'oss as ought to have won yesterday. We're goin' to see some'at seemingly," said Bulbeck, who, in spite of his fears began to feel excited and interested, "an' that's the Crier ain't it?" he queried, as the clothing was stripped off, and Cecil Warleigh throwing off his big coat, got into the saddle. "Ah, I recollect seeing him win a race two years ago at Rugby, there was four entries, I picked the Crier and another for Mr. Raggles, and I gave the other two to a young Hoxford college gent, as I used to put on to a winner every now and again."

Gipsy Joe's eyes glistened. He knew every horse in Tom Ring's stables quite as well as their trainer. "Would know 'em, made into soup," as he put it, and he recognized at once Sir Roland, and he saw what was going to be done for the tout's benefit.

"That's the winner of this year's big race at Liverpool, there ain't nothink to touch 'im across country. The best horse and the best rider in England," he said, as he peered into Bulbeck's face to see if he could detect any look of suspicion in it.

"There, you wait a bit and you'll see him leave Clovis and the other as if they were standing still, after they have been round the track about once," he added.

Clovis, the Crier, and another chestnut horse, which Mr. Bulbeck had seen win several races at Sandown, broke from a canter into a gallop. The tout had been enough on race-courses to believe that he knew something about horses galloping, and he watched them eagerly as they took the first jump that had been put up on the track. Suddenly his face twitched with excitement, and he clutched the gipsy by the arm, and pointed with a trembling finger at the horse Cecil Warleigh was riding.

"He's lame ! or I'm going stone blind.

He's lame, the Crier's lame!" Bulbeck gasped out convulsively.

"What? lame, the Crier lame? Go on with yer," snarled gipsy Joe quietly; then suddenly he said, "Blame me! my downy cove, if you bain't right though. The favourite for the Grand National lame! an' if he wins at Liverpool, I'll eat him, tail and all."

Captain Warleigh had stopped the horse and Tom Ring had got off Clovis and was examining the Crier. They were not fifty yards off, and the tout could hear a volley of expletives in full force, as Tom Ring expressed his opinion that it is a "hopeless case."

"Stoop down, man, don't let 'em know as we see'd it; or there'll be murder done. You've not come to Windmill Lodge for nothink gaffer, after all. There'll be some'at o' news for you to send up to the parties as sent yer down."

Mr. Bulbeck's face showed that he realized the position; probably no one else would know what he had found out, and that the people connected with the horse would keep its unsoundness dark, so as to save as much of their money as possible, was, according to his way of looking at things, a certainty. He realized that Warleigh and the trainer would perhaps make it very warm for him if they knew that he had pryed into their secret.

" I'm off at once, I can get out into the road without them spotting me, and then I'll hook it off like winking to the village and send a wire up to town. Don't you tell no one, an' I'll see you get a bit for this mornin's work. I'm going to send a wire up to Jimmy Grueby an' one or two more big men in the ring, who will make a lot o' money out of this," said Bulbeck, and without any more ceremony he took himself off. The gipsy watched him till he was well on his way, and then came out of the plantation and walked up to where Cecil and Tom Ring were standing.

" It's all right, Captain, he's as full of himself as a turkey-cock. He's going to wire up to Jim Grueby and several others of 'em. May-be the Crier will be knocked out of the betting this morning." Joe Lea was a very good judge of character in his rough-and-ready way, and he did not for one moment believe that Cecil Warleigh was merely playing a practical joke for its own sake in the plot he had carried out so successfully. That morning Bulbeck wired up to London that the Crier was dead lame. Cecil Warleigh had learned how to telegraph at Windmill Lodge in the old days, and as soon as he got back to the house, he sent a message off to a commissioner telling him to take any price he could get over five to one, to any amount, but to take care and not interfere till the horse had been sent down in the betting. Then after an excellent breakfast he went out hunting. Things were looking up with him, and now he almost admitted to himself that he had been tempted to find out what the good thing for the National, which Colonel Beamish had hinted at, really was. Now that temptation would be removed from him, he felt sure that he would be able to get on the Crier at a fairly remunerative price. He had a capital day's hunting, the horse he was on, one of Jack's, carried him splendidly. Nobody bothered him about the Grand National, for he came late to the meet. As he rode home he pictured to himself the state that Mr. Grueby and some of his brethren would get into after they had received the tout's telegram. Nobody else would be very anxious to take the bets they offered, for the notion that there was something wrong would spread like wild fire, and his commissioner would probably get the lion's share of the market. To tell the truth, his conscience never for one moment smote him for the trick he had played. It was quite fair play, he thought. If people sent touts to other men's training quarters it only served them right to be hoisted with their own petard.

"I doubt if Sir John would altogether like this business. He has rather a strict notion of things," Tom Ring had said to him, looking a little grave and uncomfortable; but Cecil had laughed at the idea of his nephew going so far in the indulgence of absurd scruples, as to object to a tout's being fooled. Besides, he thought to himself, there was not the slightest chance of Sir John knowing anything about it in time to in any way interfere with his plans being carried out. On coming into the sitting room he found Jack smoking a cigarette.

"Hullo! you've come back. Hope the meeting went off well."

" Well, the dinner went off well enough. I made a speech which seemed to go down, but there was no meeting this morning. Lord Whippenham had to go by an early train," Jack answered, then he hesitated, as if he had something unpleasant to say. "I say, Cecil, I heard of that business this morning, about the fellow being persuaded into thinking that

Sir Roland was the Crier. A gipsy fellow, Joe Lees, an infernally bad lot, came up and told me about it. He seemed to think it a rare joke, quite chuckling over it. I didn't know what he was driving at, at first, but I got it all out of him."

Cecil cursed inwardly at the gipsy for not keeping his mouth shut, but managed to look fairly pleasant. After all, it didn't much matter so long as the tout had sent his telegram.

"Oh, it's just a joke, that's all, to teach the fellow that he isn't so sharp as he thinks, in prying about here," he answered.

"Well, you know it occurred to me that it might be a more serious business: make a sort of mystery about the horse, and send it down in the betting. Now I hate anything of that sort about my horses."

"Oh, very little harm will be done to any one, and every one will say that if the fellow's employers do burn their fingers, it will serve them right."

"I don't suppose much harm will be done, but, just to make certain of it, as soon as I got home and I found the horse was as fit and as well as he could be, I sent off some wires to Dargle and to Bamborough, and one or two others. I told them that the report of the horse being lame was all nonsense, and that a tout had mistaken another horse for the Crier. I also sent a wire to the Victoria Club to the same effect."

Cecil did not say a word; it was creditable to his power of self-control, that he managed to keep silent.

"I thought it right to do so. I daresay it was a needless precaution, and that the joke you played would have been a harmless one enough, but the wires I sent can't do any harm."

"Harm! No, of course, no harm. You were quite right to do what you thought best," answered Cecil in a dreamy sort of way. As he spoke, a servant brought in a telegram. It was from his commissioner. "*Couldn't get on. The Crier left off at two to one,—taken,*" was how it ran.

"I am glad you don't mind," said Jack, "you see I am responsible to a certain extent for anything that goes on here, and I should not like any one to think I did anything at all shady or sharp."

"No fear of any one thinking that, my dear fellow, not the slightest," and then he relapsed into silence, and was not a particularly cheerful companion for the remainder of the evening.

CHAPTER XV.

IN WHICH TWO PEOPLE COME TO AN UNDERSTANDING.

A DAY or two after his interview with Beamish, Cecil went on leave, and on the next Sunday morning he was walking down Piccadilly, towards Kensington. Well dressed and handsome, with that healthy, open-air look about him, which is characteristic of Englishmen who are given to field sports, he seemed to be just the specimen of an English soldier one would desire to point out to the intelligent foreigner. He did not show a care, but looked well-contented with himself and the world in general. On his way he met plenty of men he knew. A great judge, who was walking eastward, brightened up when he saw him. The sight of Cecil reminded him of a week's hunting he had managed to secure that winter, and he shook hands very heartily with him, and said a word or two about the sport he loved better than any other occupation in the world. Dumberly, the barrister, who passed the two as they talked together, looked enviously at Cecil. He knew the judge privately, he was socially Cecil's equal, he had a blameless reputation, was a very sound lawyer, and a rising man; yet his lordship never showed the slightest pleasure on the rare occasions when he spoke to him. To tell the truth, there was no subject on which the learned judge cared to talk to him; for a knowledge of case law, a blameless life, and even a neat forensic wit, do not somehow by themselves make an engaging companion. Cecil Warleigh was very popular with his seniors, he reminded men of their amusements, and was a good fellow. A distinguished general shook hands with him. A member of the Government stopped to ask him about the chances of the Crier, and wished him good luck; and several younger men of fashion and position greeted him with much cordiality.

Yes, he was popular enough, he thought and somehow or other he began to indulge in a very unusual train of thought, as to his position and prospects. Many a man who was rolling in money would give a great deal to enjoy his popularity and perhaps envied him. His thoughts took a somewhat abrupt turn when he encountered Colonel Beamish, as he walked in the Park. That gentleman, gorgeously dressed, wearing a very shiny hat, very much on one side of his head, was lighting a large cigar as he strolled out through the park gates. He did not embarrass Cecil with any ostentatious greeting. He only gave a glance of recognition, such a look, thought Cecil, that a pickpocket on business would give to a brother craftsman.

Yes, if the men who knew him were only made acquainted with the details of that interview he had with Beamish, would they be quite so cordial? Well, most men had some little passages in their lives, which they would sooner keep hidden. It was a comfort anyhow to find that the Colonel had shown no intention of parading their acquaintance.

"Confounded impudent beggar, the Colonel," thought Cecil, as he remembered the way the six hundred pounds had been extracted from him. "Still he was a pretty shrewd customer. Wonder what it was at thirties to one, which he fancied so much for the Grand National. 'Thirty to one,' why a third of that price would not be so bad, if he could manage to get

it about 'The Crier;' but three to one:
that was utterly absurd.   He had to thank
that young fool Jack for the horse being
at such a ridiculous price."   Leaving the
park, he turned off to a street behind
Kensington Court, a street composed of
small houses, in one of which General
Cottingham lived.

"My father is out for the afternoon,"
Kate said, as she held out a thin white
hand for him to shake.

"Yes, I know that, I came to see you."

"I suppose I ought to be flattered, for
calls are not much in your line; but pretty
speeches are hardly necessary between us.
I think it would have been better if you
had stayed away," she answered, taking
her seat in a low wicker chair.

"Well, since I am here, you can listen
to what I want to say to you," Cecil said
in a low voice, as he looked down into her
face, which just then was set and rigid.
He longed to see it soften and brighten,
as it used to do.   Even then there was
just a ghost of the old look in her eyes.
She had never fascinated him so much.
The loose dress of some soft white
material clung to her tall, graceful figure,
and became her well.   There was an un-
wonted flush which added to the delicate
charm of her pale face.

"Well, what have you come to say?" she asked in a calm, emotionless tone.

For a second, Cecil looked into her face, as she leant her head back over the chair, something like a mocking smile flitted over it. Then before she could guess what he intended to do, he seized and held her head back, and leaning down, kissed her, again and again, on the lips. For a second or two she seemed not to struggle, then she tore herself from his hands, and springing to her feet, said :—

"How dare you insult me so? leave the room."

Cecil stood silent for a few minutes, looking ashamed of himself, then suddenly—

"It isn't the first time, you know!" he said.

"You coward, you contemptible coward, to say that to me! Now, I am glad that you came here to-day, for now I know how brutal you are, and I feel ashamed as I ought to be, that I could ever have cared for you."

"I couldn't help it, Kate! by the Lord, I couldn't. It was the way you looked up at me, and I remembered how things once were. I was a fool then and never knew how much I loved you, but you've had your revenge. I care more for you now

than ever you cared for me. And you
laugh at me. You were laughing at me
down at Fetchester, the other day when
you were carrying on with Jack.”

“I had something more to think of,
than laughing at you,” she answered.

“You were thinking of landing that
young fool. Don’t you think you might
tell me what you mean doing there ?”

“I don’t know what right you have to
ask me ; but I’ll tell you. If that ‘ young
fool ’ as you call him — because he is generous, unsuspicious and honest—asks me to
be his wife, I shall accept him. Now, say
that you’ll prevent it. Yes, I know that
you were going to say that ; you look so
ashamed of yourself.”

“ Hang it all, I’m not such a bad lot as
you seem to think me. No, I shan’t try
to prevent it. I was a fool when I gave
you up. By George ! I believe you feel
the same to me. I love you a hundred
times better now than I did then. You
would have chanced it then. Why
shouldn’t you now ? Why shouldn’t we
get married ? With you for my wife, I’d
get on somehow.’

“ I ought to feel honoured at your
offering to marry me. I should live in
barracks, and we should have your pay,
and what you could pick up at cards and

by riding races.   Or you might make a beginning by going through the Bankruptcy
Court, and having to leave the Army,"
she said, breaking out into a laugh, but
there was a note of sadness in it.

"By George ! You've altered since the
old days," Cecil said, staring blankly at
her.

"Yes, I have," she replied, "I learned
my lesson in the old days.   You taught
it me.   Don't you remember insisting how
stupid it would be for two paupers like
ourselves to get married ?   In those days,
if you had been a trooper, I would have
followed the regiment, to be your wife.
You were right, and I know it now.   I
was a fool, young as I was, not to know
that what meant everything in life to me,
then, was only amusement for you."

"Well, I loved you all the time, only I
was fool enough not to know how much.
You are not as hard as you make out.
Look me in the face, and say you don't
care one bit for me, and I'll believe it."

For a moment she seemed resolute
enough to have said it.   All at once she
broke down.

"No, Cecil ; I can't say that.   I do care
for you ; very much indeed, almost as
much as I did when I was a foolish girl,
though not in quite the same way.   I

know your character better than I did
then. If you were different, I would
gladly enough marry you as you are,
without your having a penny ; though
Heaven knows I have no sentimental
notions about despising money. I know
the wretchedness of being without it ; but
I daren't trust you, Cecil. I should know
that when you felt what it is to be hopelessly in debt, you would be sorry for it ;
and that would make me miserable."

"Well, anyhow, Kate, I know you do
care for me, and if it were possible, you
would marry me. We'll wait. Give me six
weeks, and who knows whether it won't be
possible. Promise me you won't accept
Jack before then."

"What chance can there be, Cecil? It
is cruel of you to play with me like this.
But for the time you mention it shall be so.
After that there shall never again be any
agreement or contract between you and
me."

Cecil walked back to his chambers in
Bury Street, choosing a path across the
Park where he was not likely to meet any
one he knew.

He had known Kate since she was a
long-legged little girl, running about
Barracks, when she could get away from
her governess. She had not, perhaps,

had the advantage of a very careful
bringing up. General Cottingham's
marriage had not been a very auspicious
one. It arose out of an elopement, and
only became possible after a decree
nisi.

Kate's mother died when the child was
but sixteen, and after that she was sent
to school. It was two years afterwards,
when Cecil, some ten years older than
Kate, declared that they had both made
fools of themselves, as he called it to her
face. Perhaps Kate had been, of the
pair, more in earnest, though Cecil was
harder hit than he thought for at the
time. He certainly had not taken long
to come to his senses. A serious flirtation
with General Cottingham's daughter
would be in many respects dangerous.

So he had, not over mercifully, shown the
folly of any sentiment to poor Kate, who
was made very miserable, while he had set
himself down to forget all about it. And
after all, in the end he found himself the
weaker of the two. Their positions were
reversed. She talked worldly prudence,
and he gnashed his teeth while he watched
her flirting with Jack.

" Jack ! Confound him, who has everything he wants, and is always in the way,"
Cecil thought, and then he began to spe-

culate as to what his life would have been if
he had married her, when she was so des-
perately fond of him.   Being hard up, and
all that sort of thing, was bad, but he
knew that he would now give a good
deal to have the lot he had then been
afraid of.   His circumstances were not so
desperate then, and he might have pulled
up, and got on very well, and still, after
all, she loved him.   Yes, for all her self-
restraint, she had not been able to help
showing it.   He began to think of his
circumstances, his debts, his very doubtful
prospects, and the short period of grace
which Kate had reluctantly promised him.
He was conscious of what he had
thought when he persuaded her to make
that promise, and his reflections led him
to Colonel Beamish and the conversation
they had had together after his game at
cards with Raggles.

" Depend upon it," Cecil thought, there
was something in the Colonel's notion of
the chances of an outsider for Liverpool.
He was a pretty wide-awake gentleman,
was the Colonel, and he had a very considerable respect for the judgment on turf
matters of Mr. Kit Lukes, his confederate
and ally.   Yes, it seemed the only game
on the cards.   Perhaps it was hard on
Jack, but then Jack had brought it on

himself by not keeping his mouth shut, and being so infernally in the way.

The outcome of this train of thought was that Cecil went to his club and wrote a letter to Colonel Beamish. He did not post it just then, but put it into his pocket. A characteristic little circumstance was that he removed from the blotting-pad the sheet of blotting-paper upon which he had blotted the letter and envelope, and tore it up into many pieces.

CHAPTER XVI.

DOWNHILL.

A STRONG tinge of sport hangs about Tankard's Hotel, Little Paint Street, Haymarket. The waiters at this hotel do not require to look at a time-table when they are asked by the guests as to the trains to Newmarket; for a fair proportion of the inhabitants of that trim little Cambridgeshire town put up at Tankard's when they visit the metropolis. Many of the guests have a healthy, open-air look about them, which suggests Newmarket Heath before breakfast, and lives devoted to the race-horse in training. Jockeys and trainers affect Tankard's, so do a select circle of the ringmen. In fact, it is a great resort of the professionals of the turf.

The night porter habitually wears a troubled expression. It is caused by his in vain trying to reconcile the various items of turf information which he obtains "straight" from the most reliable quarters. He knows a deal too much, what with what one party and another tells him. This is his sad complaint on the morrow after some classic race.

"*The party as owns the winner*," he will say, "was a staying here three weeks ago, and one night, when he comes home a little in liquor, he begs an˙ implores me to back it. 'Pogson,' he says, 'whatever you does, and whatever you leaves undone, have a good bit on 'my horse.' But bless me, there I goes and lets a party from Stockbridge talk me into havin' all my little bit o' money on the favourite. I hear so much from so many different parties, that it drives me nearly wild."

The smoking room at Tankard's is a well known resort of turfites. Of an evening the conversation at most of the tables relates to racing. The coppers given to the waiters, as a rule, help to make up the modest little sum for which they back the opinion they have formed after tips from various gentlemen who use the room and ought to know something. When they bring the whiskies and water, and the gins and soda, which are great drinks at Tankard's, they will indulge the guests with mysterious conversation about parties who "got on at *sixty-sixes* and stood it all without hedging a penny piece."

There is one white-haired old gentleman, sometimes joined by a friend, who uses the corner seat of the corner-box near the fire, who is said to be allured by the excellence of the brandy and water, though he had the utmost detestation for the turf and all who follow it. Certainly he never joins in the conversation on the subject, and when he hears it being carried on in his box, a look of disgust comes over his face. It is a favourite jest of the choice spirits of Tankard's to impart information on future events to him, which he will receive with contempt and loathing—or to treat him as one, who if he only cared to talk, could unfold turf secrets which would make the fortunes of the room. Tankard's was much affected by Colonel Beamish. He was thoroughly at home in the society to be met there. He belonged to a Club, a proprietary institution, owned by a speculative and frequently bankrupt wine merchant, which had a committee of well known names, who had never been inside the door of the Club, and a list of members which included the flower of the sixty-per-centers and various great men in Israel, who it is said would meet there on their Sabbath, to compare notes as to whose paper was out. But Colonel Beamish found himself far more at home at Tankard's. Kit Lukes, the lawyer, occasionally looked in there, and he would meet the book-makers and money-lenders, who formed the bulk of his legal connection.

About a week after that game of poker which ended so disastrously for Mr. Raggles, Mr. Lukes and the Colonel were there, and at the same table sat another man with whom they were talking in a low tone with considerable earnestness. Their companion was a man whose appearance at first sight was decidedly in his favour. There was a look of good breeding about the well-cut features of his thin face, and a grace in his long lithe limbs, in the slight tilt of his well made billycock hat which bore signs of much weather, and in the cut of his suit of homespun, there was a strong suggestion of the stable, but for all that one would feel but little doubt that he was a gentleman by birth. As one grew accustomed to his looks they did not improve. That good-looking face would meet your gaze straightly enough, but a doubt of his honesty grew upon one, though one recognized that he had plenty of pluck.

As he talked to Lukes and Beamish, the pleasing, happy-go-lucky expression he usually wore, altered to one of annoyance, and he seemed to be anything but best pleased with his companions. "Hang it, I tell you I can beat the Crier," he was saying. "It is not a certainty, but it's the next best thing to it. And yet here is Lukes without the pluck to risk it. We shall never have a better chance, nor one where we can win so much money. Half the men in town are crazy to back the Crier. Gad! I'd like 'em to see the little mare coming in first. Whose is it, they will ask, and they'll be told it's Pat Considine's, Lord Dargle's brother, whom they have thought fit to cut any time these ten years. Dargle will be wild. He's going to back the Crier, hang him. I hope it will break him. The last time I met him was at Mallet's Hotel, in the coffee-room, and seeing me he said, ' Come, clear out, Pat, this room's not big enough for me and you. Go and get a drink in the sort of company you're fit for,' and he threw five shillings on the table, just as if I were a groom; I'd like to have knocked the teeth down his throat, curse him."

" But you didn't, Pat, and you stuck to the five shillings, I'd like to back the double event," said Mr. Lukes.

" No, faith, I saw he'd have liked me to have thrown it back at him, and felt he was spending too much in insulting me. It's not often one gets any coin out of Dargle, but the book-makers will, if we only beat the Crier. He'll be hit hard, and so will many another man I hate ; but there you won't risk it."

" 'I bide my time,' that's some swell's motto. I saw it in the Peerage the other day. By George ! it's a precious good one for the turf. I wait till it's a certainty, if I have to wait another two years," said Mr. Lukes.

" I am of Pat's way of thinking," said Beamish. *Another year !* Why, where mayn't we all be in another year ? Dead or in prison."

" Speak for yourself, Colonel. For a distinguished military man, you have a curious way of talking," answered Mr. Lukes. " I shan't be dead, I hope, and I certainly shall not be in prison, unless the company I keep deteriorates my character a good deal."

" Dashed if I don't run my horse though, and if you don't think it good enough, back something else. I shan't be any the less pleased to win on that account," said Pat, paying no attention to Lukes' remark to his partner.

"Suppose the horse comes in second to the Crier," answered Lukes, "good-bye to the chance of ever bringing off a big *coup*. No, you won't do that, Pat, my boy, for you see, she isn't *altogether* yours."

"*Pat, my boy!* It's a nice state of things when you talk like that to Lord Dargle's brother. But I'll get out of your hands, Mr. Lawyer Lukes, settle that bill of sale, and then it won't be 'Pat, my boy,' to me from you."

"Better be called Pat by me than number so-and-so by a warder at Portland," whispered Mr. Lukes, with a malicious twinkle in his eyes. "If you get out of my hands, may-be you'll get into worse," he added aloud. "Why ain't we in the same boat? Do you think it any great hardship to have to give in to Kit Lukes' opinion on a matter like this? Ask the cleverest man you know on the turf whether it is."

"You may be clever enough, Kit, but we are not in the same boat. I want to win some money at once. Who knows what may happen in a year? The mare may have gone wrong, and she will never be as fit as she will be in a month's time. You'd be of my opinion if you'd ridden her as I have," said Pat.

" I say you're both right. · Dash down the money at once and make a certainty of it," said Beamish. "Now, I've a notion."

" We'll hear it when you're sober, Colonel," said Lukes, kicking at Beamish under the table. " Well, I can't make up my mind what we'll do. But we'll be down at Broxton to-morrow evening, and next morning we will see what Blue Ruin can do, so you had better keep straight and fit."

" If I were your trainer instead of a man of family, who owns a racehorse, you couldn't be more arbitrary. But I say, how are you fellows off for chips ? I was not able to draw some coin to-day ; and I want a fiver to take me down to Broxton."

" Three sovs. will have to do you," said Lukes, giving him the coin, and entering the amount in his pocket-book.

The Honourable Pat fingered the coins in his pocket and then made a hurried adieu.

" Mind you get home soon and look after yourself and Blue Ruin," said Lukes, as Pat left. " Not much chance of his staying away long though, with only three sovs. to spend," he added to Beamish who was glaring at him angrily.

" What do you mean by speaking to

me like that, before Pat Considine, '*Wait till I'm sober.*' Indeed, it's lucky for you I am sober. I'd have taken a fancy to see what a lawyer with the life-half-knocked-out-of-him is like."

"A devilish dangerous customer even then you'd find. But never mind your bluster. I didn't want you to talk before him. I thought may-be you were going to say something that it would be as well not to say before Pat."

"I wonder you trust that man as you do. You're about the only man on the turf who would."

"I trust him, though he would take any one else in, but he daren't be crooked with me. I've got a hold over him. Not only that I could have him warned off the turf. Pretty nearly every one knows that much about him. But there's something more awkward. That's the sort I like to deal with. I trust them."

"You'd like to have such a hold over me, wouldn't you? asked Beamish, looking into the other's fat face. "But by —— you'd find it dangerous if you had. I'd sooner be in the condemned cell than in your power."

"Talk sense, man! What were you going to say just now?"

"I was going to say that if the Crier could be made a 'stiff 'un,' we'd have as good a chance this year as ever."

"And who is he to be 'got at' through?" asked Mr. Lukes with a sneer. "Sir John Warleigh or Tom Ring, his trainer?"

"Not the owner or the trainer, but what would you say about the rider?"

"Captain Warleigh! Why, that you didn't know your man. What on earth makes you think you could come to terms with him?"

"Well, it happens I do know my man. I know a good bit more about him than any of his swell friends do. And I know he won't stick at a trifle."

"But 'stopping' the horse he rides for the Grand National and letting in Sir John, who I happen to know has been a very good friend to him, is a good bit more than a trifle. No, Colonel, I don't believe he'd do it. You don't quite understand what it is for a man like that, who has a character to lose, to do a thing of that sort. It's just a *leetle* too strong."

"Perhaps you'd be surprised to hear what I do know about the Captain. It's between pals, Kit, now listen to this."

And Beamish, with considerable satisfaction, related the story of the game of poker.

Mr. Lukes listened attentively. "Well, I always thought he was a pretty shrewd customer, but never knew he'd go quite that length. Still, rooking a young ass like Raggles is one thing, and letting in Sir John and all his swell friends who are backing the horse, is another. If he does, he'll want to get a good lot out of it."

"He'll set your mind at rest about that—Hullo! a letter for me. Shouldn't be surprised if it is from him—By George! I'm right—it is," said the Colonel, as he tore open a letter the waiter brought him. "Well, what do you say to that? Read it."

"Wants to see you—will be in his chambers, Bury Street, to-night after eleven—or any other evening. H'm! well, it looks like business. Strike while the iron is hot, Colonel. Go and see him, and if there's business in it, he can come down with us to-morrow, and see what Blue Ruin can do."

"He won't like meeting you and Pat; he will feel a little shy at first."

"He'll have to get over his shyness as far as I'm concerned, that's all I've got to say. When I do business of that sort, I treat with the party in person. As for Pat, he need not see him or know anything about it. Put it to him pretty short : that if he sees his way to working with us, he can come down to Broxton to-morrow, and have a look at the mare. As you two are old pals, I'll keep out of it at present ; but if it comes to business, he'll have to arrange matters with Mr. Christopher Lukes, solicitor, and there must be no nonsense."

" All right, my limb of the law, I'll do the *suaviter in modo.* Last time I had to touch him up a bit with the *fortiter in re*, and I think you'll allow, Mr. Kit, that I did know my man. By George ! when I saw him rooking that young flat, I was thinking all the time of the favourite beat at Liverpool, and the Honourable Pat on little Blue Ruin, coming in alone," said the Colonel, as he swaggered off, thinking that he had taught the lawyer that he was not to be sneered at as a confederate.

Cecil Warleigh's chambers suggested that their owner had tastes somewhat superior to those which he would have been credited with. There were several very good engravings on the walls. A statuette or two on brackets, that must have cost a deal of money : while on the book-shelves, among sporting works and French novels, there were some books on history and politics, and a classical author or two, which told that he now and then indulged in hard reading.

Cecil was sitting back in an arm-chair, smoking a cigarette, with a soda and brandy on a table by his side, to which he had frequent recourse, as he nervously watched the clock.

"He may be here soon," he said to himself. "If he got the note he wouldn't be long coming, for he seemed anxious enough to get me into his clutches ; confound him !" Just then there was a knock at the door, and an attendant, to whom he had given strict orders that he was "not at home" to any one but Colonel Beamish, announced that gentleman.

"Well, Captain, so the youngster weighed in all right with his cheque. And now you want to know how to invest it ? Don't see your way to popping it down on the Crier at seven to four ?" said the Colonel, after the servant had left the room, and he had mixed a brandy and soda. "You think there's a better game than that, eh, my young sharp ?" he went on.

Cecil winced at the other's manner, but did not show his disgust. "It depends upon whether there is anything else worth backing. Two to one *is* a short price. If there had not been so much talk, it wouldn't have been anything like so short."

"Sir John will learn some day, that if he opens his mouth on the turf, he will have the gold taken out of his eye teeth. But as for whether there is anything else worth backing. If you are game for a trip down to Broxton, you shall see what you shall see, and after that, we will have a bit of a talk."

"Whom shall I meet there?" asked Cecil.

"No one except me and Kit Lukes. Not another soul need know you've been down there. You can drop down by Newspaper train, and get back to town again before Friday."

"Kit Lukes!" said Cecil in a tone of aversion, for something seemed to tell him that dealings with that gentleman were dangerous.

"Yes, Kit Lukes, you and me. There will only be three of us regularly in the swim," said Beamish.

"It is a nice partnership for a gentleman to join!" said Cecil, half inclined at the last moment to give the whole thing up.

The Colonel laughed merrily.

" You'll find it a fairly profitable one, and we keep our mouths shut."

" Well, I didn't send for you to make a fool of you, I will come down all right," answered Cecil.

When Beamish left, Cecil sat for some hours smoking and staring into the fire. Promises of youth that had come to nothing—temptations that had been yielded to—shady transactions that had escaped punishment, and ceased to trouble him—such memories as these passed across his memory. Bah ! what did it matter ? How many of the men who would cut him if he were found out, would really think much the worse of him if they found out what he was going to do and were certain that no one else shared the secret ? What would nine out of ten of them do ? Why, lay against the Crier, keep their mouths shut, and remain his very good friends.

CHAPTER XVII.

ON THE HAMPSHIRE DOWNS.

"There is the winner of the Grand National, Captain Warleigh, and it's not been quoted in the betting but once or twice, and that at forty to one. The Honourable Pat Considine's Blue Ruin, they call her, but I don't mind saying that she is practically owned by your humble servant and our friend Beamish."

Kit Lukes had pulled up his dog-cart under Broxton Hanger, so as to get some shelter from the wind which swept keenly across the stretch of Hampshire Downs. From where they were they had a good view of the private steeple-chase course which Nick Holmes had put up near his stables. A string of horses were being walked across the flat between the stables and the course, while over the crest of the Down a man on a horse had come in sight, to which Lukes pointed with his whip as he spoke.

It was only eight o'clock on a winter's morning, but the lawyer had on his company manners. The rôle he played on such occasions was that of a hearty John Bullish, frank fellow. His manner, however, was wasted on Cecil Warleigh, who, huddled up in a huge ulster, looked moody and out of spirits.

"Pat Considine! The less one has to do with that young gentleman the better. I don't want to meet him," growled Cecil, and he pushed a soft hat he was wearing further over his face.

"So you don't like Master Pat? I am afraid he is not quite the clean potato; perhaps though he's not so black as he's painted; but he's sure not to see you."

That Pat Considine, whom he had cut years before, should know that he was mixed up with such characters as Beamish and Lukes! And the prospect of being welcomed as a chum and confederate by him seemed worse even than to be cut and shunned by honourable men.

"Well, he can ride, I will say that for him," said Cecil. Then continuing—"So Blue Ruin is the wonder? I fancy I have seen her before: at Sandown, I think, last year, but she hasn't done anything lately."

"No, and won't till she brings off a big

cup. I have the management of her.
You'll see presently how smart she is.
One can't try 'em across country as you
can on the flat, but those fences ain't so
unlike what she'll have to negotiate at
Liverpool: while as for the difference of
the ground, that'll all be in favour of the
mare. She takes to 'plough' wonderfully."

"Hullo, there's the tout-eater," said
Beamish, who was in the back seat, as
they heard the baying of a big hound
coming from the direction of the stables
at the foot of the hill. "That's the
brute they kicked up the row about. He
ate a good bit of a horse-watcher, who
was hiding in the furze yonder, waiting
to see a trial."

"Yes, and they had to pay the widow
and orphans a good bit of money; but
it paid 'em in the end. None of
the touting fraternity have much to say
about Nick Holmes' lot," answered
Lukes.

"What's Holmes got out to-day?
Jack Shepherd and Old Clo. Hang me, if
I don't love Jack. I've won a lot by him
one way and another."

"Most of it *in another*," said Beamish,
alluding possibly to the occasions when
that horse had been laid against by his

own party—and the two partners joined in a laugh.

Cecil felt that they were making no stranger of him. He hardly relished the compliment.

"He's a good horse though, and fit as a fiddle. Young Holmes is on Jack Shepherd. Now, you'll see what Blue Ruin is made of. She goes over her fences like a cat," said Beamish, after Pat Considine had come up to the others, and they had started together at a good striding pace.

"She is smart, uncommon smart," said Cecil through his clenched teeth, as he watched the gallant little grey mare, Jack Sheppard and Old Tom.

"Well, Captain, that is our trump card," said Kit Lukes, coming back to the dog-cart and hoisting himself in. "They're at level weights this morning; but Blue Ruin is in the National at 10 st. 7 lbs., and what would they say to Jack Shepherd at 11 st. ? I fancy that he'd have a very fair chance."

"Not against the Crier, he wouldn't," said Cecil.

"Well, Jack ain't first chop, but he's pretty near as good as anything else, bar Blue Ruin and the Crier. See there, the mare is a different class altogether."

Neither of them spoke, but watched the horses intently; but Cecil's thoughts to a certain extent even then dwelt on the plot that he was required to take part in. He saw how good the mare seemed to be, he realized the grand *coup* that could be brought off, if the Crier was not to win.

Kit Lukes every now and then took a stealthy glance into his face, as if he would tell what he was thinking of. " Look at her now, why, Jack Sheppard can't make her gallop."

" Now they have done three miles," cried Beamish, as the horses galloped by them for the third time : Blue Ruin with a lead of some three lengths. " And mind you, she's in at 10-7 lbs. ; Pat can ride that weight, and next to yourself he's as good as any one."

" Better. If he wouldn't be up to any of his tricks," said Cecil, and then he looked rather uncomfortable, as he thought that he wouldn't have much right in the future to cast the stones which he had been in the habit of throwing at that not over-reputable young gentleman.

" Pat doesn't try his tricks with me," answered Lukes rather grimly.

" You are right, she's smart enough, better fencer than Jack Sheppard, and a lot faster," remarked Cecil as the little mare finished some dozen lengths in front of the others.

"And she's hardly been mentioned in the betting," said Beamish.

"And now the sooner we get to work at the breakfast I've ordered at the Station Hotel, the better I shall be pleased. This morning air makes one feel as if one could pick up a crumb," said Mr. Lukes, as he turned the horse round and drove off at a brisk pace.

The landlord had, as Mr. Lukes said, done very well for them : and they sat down to a very excellent breakfast in the snug coffee-room, embellished with coloured engravings of some of the great race-horses that had been trained on the far-famed Downs of which there was a fine view from the window. Even Cecil, who was inclined to be moody and disconsolate, felt a good deal better after some capital trout, a rasher of bacon, some fresh poached eggs, and a plate of pigeon pie.

" Bless me, what a good fellow I should be if I only lived in the country, and ate a breakfast like this every day of the week ! I feel at peace and charity with all men," said Mr. Lukes, after he had filled his pipe and poured out a glass of sparkling home-brewed ale. "And now, Captain Warleigh, we'll talk business," and as he spoke his whole manner altered. "I take it, Captain, that you mean business, and are willing to work with us for the Grand National?"

"Yes, I do mean business, that is, if you think this Blue Ruin is good enough to win," replied Cecil, and as he spoke a feeling akin to relief came over him. He was in for it now. He, Cecil Warleigh, was working with Beamish, the mysterious colonel, and Kit Lukes, the shady turf lawyer. From henceforth they were to be his accomplices and allies. It was true that he would go on living in the same society of men of honour and gentlemen ; but he would really belong to the other side, and be with, not of the men he saw most of.

"Well, she's certain to beat any, bar yours. I believe it's a rare good thing, and she's at 33 to 1."

Warleigh looked steadily into the lawyer's face. Cunning low scoundrel though he knew he was, he was a rare judge of racing, and though he would have poisoned the best horse that ever was foaled, he had the instincts of a sportsman, though he could not often afford to indulge them.

"Pat Considine says she'll beat the Crier at the weights, she's only got 10st. 7lb. to carry. I think she can beat anything bar the Crier. Now the question is, can we lay the Crier?"

"What can we hope to make out of it?" asked Cecil, answering one question by another.

Kit Lukes went into figures. Calculating how much they could lay against the favourite, and how much they could back the outsider for.

"We could get about twelve thousand, say, out of the Crier, for it is a good-betting race, and could back Blue Ruin to win—say, thirty thousand, nibbling at her a little, and putting a lump on at the start. Pat Considine would want a little, and we could divide the rest. Say, twelve thousand apiece."

"Six thousand is more than Pat Considine has had for a long time," said Cecil—"and mind he knows nothing about my being in this."

"Nothing—not that you need be afraid of master Pat Considine talking about my business. And now, Captain, let's look at the other side. How much we stand to lose? Before I execute this commission I would like to have some sort of security that you don't forget all about the arrangement when it comes to the race."

"Hang it all, don't you trust a gentleman?" asked Cecil.

"Not to go straight in a swindle," answered Lukes, and then followed a little confidential talk about securities, and authority in writing being given to Lukes. It ended in Cecil Warleigh knowing that he had hopelessly given his honour away, and would have to do Kit Lukes' work, or be ruined in pocket and reputation.

"Hullo! Warleigh, my boy, fancy meeting you. And what has brought you into this part of the world?" said a voice in a suppressed Dublin brogue, from the corner of the first-class carriage into which Cecil jumped, after having taken leave of Lukes and Beamish at the hotel; those worthies deeming it better to wait for the next train to avoid any chance of meeting people whose suspicions might be aroused by seeing them together. And Cecil had gladly fallen into this suggestion.

In the owner of the voice which had addressed him, he recognized a Dr. Buckeen, at one time the doctor of the Loyal Lancers: who having married the opulent widow of a gin-distiller, had left the Army Medical Staff, and gone on the turf.

Cecil did not answer the question, but settled himself into the corner of the carriage.

" And what brings you down to Broxton ? " asked Buckeen. " Is it Pat Considine you have been giving a look up ? "

" I have not the honour of Mr. Pat Considine's acquaintance," replied Cecil.

" Ah, well, I'm afraid he's a shocking young blackguard. Many is the time that Dargle, with tears in his eyes, has told me what a sorrow Pat has been to him. We are like brothers, Dargle and me. In fact, I'm a kind of cousin of his. But where have you been ? Have you been having a look at Nick Holmes' lot ? "

Cecil grunted out a negative as he lit a cigar.

" Ah, now I thought I caught sight of that beggar Kit Lukes and Beamish— ' Colonel ' he calls himself—but I'm thinking he's not a colonel at all. You hadn't been with them, I suppose ? "

" What the deuce has that to do with you ? " Cecil began to blurt out, but at once realized that showing temper would only make Buckeen suspicious that there was something going wrong : so he finished his reply more amiably by saying that it was Beamish that he had seen at the hotel, and he believed that Kit Lukes was with him. " I believe they train with Nick Holmes," he added.

" 'Deed they do," said Buckeen, "and talking about training, what are you going to do at Liverpool? . . . As an old friend, ought I to back the Crier ? "

" I'd like to see you back it, to win you a pot of money. I'm well on, myself ; got on at good odds," said Cecil ; the first part of his speech being far more true than the second.

Dr. Buckeen expressed his thanks, and then as the train slackened speed, he got his things together, and to Cecil's delight prepared to jump out at the next station.

When Cecil was left to himself he laughed aloud. He lit another cigarette, inhaling the smoke, and blowing it out of his mouth again, in a succession of rings.

Some of Cecil's friends noticed that he was rather excited that day, and a story was wildly told of his having backed the Crier for a large sum a day or two before, when the horse had gone down in the betting. He spoke about the race more unguardedly than he usually did. The

Crier was a wonder. A giant in the days of dwarfs. A horse that could have held his own in the palmy days of cross-country racing. He had backed it for all he could afford. In fact for a little more. "He would have to lay some of it off," he told several men.

"I have never seen Warleigh like this before. I fancy he has taken an extra glass or two of champagne at dinner," said Brown to Jones at the club.

"Fancy he has backed it for more than he can afford to lose. But I shall have my modest bit on," answered Jones.

And in consequence of Cecil's talk, a good deal of money went on the Crier.

There was a ball given that evening by the wife of a man who had been in his regiment. Balls were not much in his line as a rule, but at half-past eleven Cecil jumped into a cab and was driven to Kensington.

There were a good many of his brother officers, and plenty of other men he knew in the room, and it was all the same story, —"How about the Crier?"

Cecil answered as a man does who is in a position to do his friends a good turn. It was as near a certainty as a steeple-chase could be. It was a short price, two to one, but short odds was better than losing, and he did not seem to see how the Crier could lose, provided he stood up.

"You think it good enough for me to have my last hundred on. I shall be dead broke, if it doesn't come off," said Brookes of the regiment, a reckless young subaltern whom he had always rather liked.

"I have never known anything seem such a certainty. All I have in the world is on it," said Cecil.

Poor young Brookes, he was sorry for him, but if he wanted anything to be made public property, the best thing he could do would be to tell it to him. And he did want it to be published that he had a lot of money on the Crier.

But it was not to talk about the Crier that he had gone to Mr. Barrington's ball, a proceeding which was rather out of his way as he did not generally go much into society.

Standing in the doorway, he watched the dancers and saw Kate Cottingham and Jack, standing talking to each other. They neither seemed to be very energetic dancers, but appeared to have a great deal to talk about. "She's able to twist the young ass round her fingers. She's not the prettiest girl in the room by a long bit; in fact, she's hardly pretty at

all," he thought as he watched the changing expressions of her face, and the smile
play round the lips, which now looked so
enticing, and then would become hard
and rigid.

"What the deuce is it about her that
constitutes the charm?" he asked himself.
And yet for all his thirty years, his experience, and his far more accurate knowledge of her character, he knew that she
could make a bigger fool of him than of
his nephew. A few minutes afterwards
he was sitting out a dance with her. Of
course her card was full, and equally of
course she found no difficulty in giving
him the dance he wanted.

"Why did you come here to-night?
There seems to be a fate in it. In another
half hour everything would have been
settled. I felt it was coming, and then,
before I saw you, I seemed to know that
you were here, and then it was of no
use."

"Then I am glad I came as soon as I
did, Kate. You said the other day that
you'd chance it, and take me. I am
going to claim your promise."

"Cecil, are you in earnest? But I
remember I made a condition."

"You said, Kate, that if I could show
you that I could pay my debts and start

with five hundred a year of my own, you'd
chance it. Never mind how, but in a
month's time I shall have got enough for
that."

"Cecil, I'm sure it will end miserably,
as I daresay we deserve it should : but I
am happy," she whispered, looking into
Cecil's face as they walked back into the
dancing-room ; and as he felt the pressure
of her fingers on his arm, and drank
in the yearning look of her eyes, he
felt that she was worth risking anything
for.

CHAPTER XVIII.

GRUB STREET.

MR. BINGS, the landlord of the Blue Boar, a public-house in the Bloomsbury district of the metropolis, has often expressed his opinion to the effect that genius, though all very well in one who has not got to make a living by it, doesn't sit very well on a poor man.

"There's a deal too much of it hanging about my house, bless yer, the time was when I'd listen to the jaw of the parties as use my best bar, and get took with it to the extent of almost asking 'em what they'd take to drink. I'm about sick on 'em now. They stand up and jabber away about po'try or 'istry, or politics or anythink, and take a couple of 'ours over one 'arf pint, awaitin' all the time for some one to drop in and stan' 'em drinks, till at larst they'd 'ook it off in disgust, an' go to bed, leastwise them as had beds to go to. No, genius is a loafin' lot, and that's the long an' the short on't."

Mr. Bings probably somewhat over-estimated the mental gifts of certain of his customers whom he had found in his bar when he first took the house, and whose patronage he continued to keep, though he had become by no means jealous of it. His house was one of call for a section of the outside fringe of literature.

Grub Street, we are told, is a thing of the dead past.

A few hours spent at the "Blue Boar" might possibly suggest that, somewhere or other, that locality could still be found. A nice snug little dinner with Mr. Gripps, the proprietor and editor of various periodicals with a large circulation, should that highly respectable gentleman take —as he sometimes did—enough port wine to make him confidential on the subject of how the publishing business can be made to pay, would throw further light on this interesting point. Mr. Gripps is as rigid an adherent to the doctrine of supply and demand as any Whitechapel sweater.

He believes in getting the article his public will read, on the lowest possible terms.

" Sometimes I pays nothink, but generally I gives 'em a bit ; it's cheaper in the end to pay a bit ; anyhow one has to pay one's printer, and a little money paid to a hauthor 'elps the circulation. They come to me, and I looks at their stuff and sees how much there is, an' makes a bargain with 'em, and then and there pays up.   It don't make no great hole in the profits, what I gives 'em, but it's everything to them poor devils, an' it's a charity to pay up at once."

He is not a highly educated man, is Mr. Gripps, but he knows one Latin proverb, " *Bis dat qui cito dat.*"   He beats his contributors down to their lowest figure, and then tempts them by the offer of ready money to take half.

A good many men who haunt the bar of the " Blue Boar " have dealings with Mr. Gripps, and a large proportion of the money he chucks to his authors finds its way into Mr. Bings' till. They write original stories, which they find in volumes of forgotten magazines at the library of the British Museum. They patch together scientific articles and moral essays, and before now, tempted by the thought of half-crowns which Mr. Gripps jingles in his pockets as he bargains with them—some of them have brought and sold to him really good work. To do Mr. Gripps justice, he has always on such rare occasions been quite ignorant of the value of what he bought so cheaply ; in fact he has never had any other ambition than to get the indifferent matter he wants, at its lowest possible price. There are some who do not even work for Mr. Gripps. How they live is a London mystery. You may see them at the British Museum dully droning over books they never really read, thinking, it is to be hoped for their sakes, of nothing at all but perhaps—heaven help them—of the hopes they once cherished, and of the friends who once believed in their ability and their future, but have since turned their backs upon them.

This last class, strangely enough, are those of whose genius Mr. Bings has, in a way, as high an estimate as he has a low one of their eligibility as customers to a publican.

Sam Paradine had for years been a constant frequenter of the " Blue Boar," and was perhaps the only one of the set for whom the landlord still retained much respect. Mr. Bings would sometimes not only ask him what he would have, but he has been known to lend him a few shillings, and even to go as far as to let him stand in with him in some turf transaction, to the extent on one occasion of half-a-sovereign. " He's capital company is Mr. Paradine," the landlord would say to his wife, "and has a powerful sight of hinformation ; " the only pity was that he didn't seem able to do much with it all. And on this he and his better half were agreed, for Mrs. Bings—who was even more opposed than her husband to the "literary tone" of the "Blue Boar," woman-like, being keenly alive to the shabby wearing apparel, doubtful linen and constant impecuniosity of the gentlemen who came there—made an exception of Sam, whom she admitted was "a very pleasant-spoken gentleman."

There was a corner of the bar to which he had gained a prescriptive right where he would sit with his old high hat tilted forward, and his hands—when they were not lifting the glass—pushed deeply into the pockets of his trousers. He was sitting there one afternoon when there was a gathering of some of the leading members of the "Blue Boar" set.

There was no appreciative stranger present, and in consequence the meeting gazed sadly at empty pint pots and glasses, and Mr. Bings behind the bar eyed them with an unconcealed contempt.

"Say what you like," said one of the party—a young man some years younger than the others, who had only just taken to the "Blue Boar," and hadn't realized how hopeless he had thereby made his chances of doing any good; for a moral dry rot hung about the place, as sewer gas does in the hotels of some continental health resorts,—"it is a noble ambition to appeal to thousands of readers, to write for the masses, and to cheer their toilsome lives."

"To talk dashed nonsense! Look here, youngster, keep that sort of rot for the next tea-party at Peckham Rye you are asked to, and don't talk it to us, till you've been through the mill, as we have. No sir, the one regret of my life is not that I went to grief in the army—that was a moral certainty all along, and I had my fling—but that afterwards I took to writing, instead of billiard-marking, and didn't find out what a rotten game it is, until I had held a pen so long, that I had forgotten how to use a cue. I wish I had taken to anything else, driving a hearse, going as a mute, any dashed thing!" said a shabby man with a twisted gray moustache, who was attempting to re-light the end of a cigar.

"It's a case of drinks round, Green, my boy," said Sam Paradine, regarding the young man with a look of reproach. "You can't expect to talk like that to us unless you hire the hall."

The youngster felt in all his pockets and looked nervously around.

"Ah! if that's what's the matter, my boy, we'll excuse you, and if you can get much comfort out of talking rot, and thinking rot, hanged if I grudge it you," said the man with the twisted moustache. Then there was silence, and Mr. Bings cleared away the glasses.

"Tommy Rogers' story is in the number of 'The Bohemian' that came out to-day," said the young man who had first spoken. "I saw it at a News-room."

"How much of it is there now? pages, I mean," said a man with a mouth like a pike, who sat leaning on the bar, chewing the end of a match.

"About twenty, I believe," said the young man, somewhat perplexed at the interest which his questioner took in such a minor point as the exact length of their mutual friend's production. The man chewing the match got up, growling out a "Good-bye," and left the room.

"You are a flat, Green. Why on earth should you blurt it out before that fellow Bolster? Why, as soon as he hears it, he's off to hunt up poor Tommy Rogers, and you bet he'll find him. He'll find out if he has been to the office to draw his cheque, and if he hasn't, he will hang around till he comes. They pay the day the story appears. He don't know much about literature, does Mr. Bolster, but he knows that much, and he's always hanging about on pay-day," said Captain Bashford, the military gentleman. " Tommy will draw a tenner, and Bolster will probably borrow a sovereign, and prevent Tommy coming in here. Confound him."

" Tommy is getting on. Let's see, ' The Bohemian ' is one of the things old Gripps has, isn't it ? " asked Sam Paradine. " I've forgotten what things the old beggar does own, it's a long time since I did any work for him."

" Yes, you've quite cut scribbling, Sammy, better luck for you, if you can do anything at your new game."

" There's a fortune in it," answered Sam with an air of assurance, which quite took Bashford, for it seemed so real. " If," he added mournfully, " I could get a capitalist, some one with just a little money who would finance a real good thing.

The expression of interest faded away from the faces of those present. They knew of so many fortunes which were sticking out for the poor capitalist,—plays which could be brought out, which would secure unprecedented success ; notions to be carried out for newspapers, which must succeed from the very first; books that could be published which must take the town by storm; and many other ventures in literature, journalism, and art.

"It's a book, you know, 'Old Families,' or something of that sort we'd call it, and we'd invent pedigrees for all the subscribers to the work, and then we'd go into the other's pedigrees and pull 'em to bits, and expose all the humbug of the thing; as one who has the making of pedigrees, like I have, can do. Subscribers could have the privilege of correcting anything. Mark my words, there's a pot of money in it."

"Been almost played out, I fancy. Besides, people don't care about pedigrees nowadays. Look at me, I am the head of one of the oldest families in the West of England, and Bings there won't give me a pint of beer on tick."

Bings paid no attention to this remark.

"There is money to be made out of pedigree-hunting for all that, though very little of it has come my way yet. It's better than writing for Gripps. Then there is my other game, mining in the Record Office."

"How do you work that, Samuel?"

" Well, you know, there are thousands of pounds in Chancery. Most of it will never come out, for though it belongs to some one or other, no one can find out to whom, or else there are such a lot to divide it, that it wouldn't pay expenses. But money has been got out before now. I take my case very much as the gold-digger takes his claim, with very little to tell me whether it is likely to prove payable or not. I get the papers at the Record Office, and try to find out if there are any representatives of the parties alive who have a right to it."

" Have you got much out, Sammy ? "

" No, up to date we've drawn blank. Either I couldn't make head or tail out of the papers, or I couldn't find representatives, or there were such a lot of them, that the fund came to about half-a-crown all round, but I've worked up rather a promising looking case just now. A little fund of 200*l*., and matters appear to be fairly plain-sailing."

" Very nice little fund. Wish I had as many pence. Well, I suppose Tommy Rogers won't be coming in here," said Bashford, as he lounged into the street.

Sam Paradine gave the fortunate Tommy Rogers another ten minutes or so, and finding further waiting useless, made his way into the street, bound for the reading-room at the Record Office ; where he was soon immersed in some faded old law papers, the records in the forgotten administration suit of Smith v. Matterson.

CHAPTER XIX.

DIGGING IN THE RECORD OFFICE.

IT had happened that after Sam's smash at Oxford, a relation, who was a prosperous London solicitor, had given him a chance, by taking him into his office as a clerk, with a promise of giving him his articles, if he conducted himself with propriety there.

The chance had come to nothing. Sam entered on his new duties with considerable enthusiasm. He had gone pretty straight for some months, but at the end of that time he had broken out again. The dissipations open to a lawyer's clerk with very little money in his pocket, were humbler than those of an undergraduate —with that almost unlimited credit which confiding tradesmen, in Sam's time, gave to nearly every member of the University. But such as they were, Sam adapted himself to them. In that way he had always shown great adaptability.

The consequence was that Sam and his prosperous relative had parted. The latter only consented to make the trifling loan which, on his dismissal, Sam, with a fine sense of making the best use of every one, had asked for, on the distinct understanding that he should never see or hear of him again.

After that, he had tried various ways of making a living. He had written stories for a cheap magazine, articles for papers of various views, poetry for an advertising tailor, original sermons for an ambitious young clergyman, who hoped to become a popular preacher ; and did so, though he had no brains, and only a fine voice and a good presence to work with. He had " just not succeeded " again and again. Once he almost got a berth as a political lecturer, and he had shown himself to be a very fair speaker, but an unfortunate occasion came, when he was to speak at a country meeting, and an enthusiastic politician had invited him to dine that evening. He had proved capital company at the dinner, his speech at the meeting had been the cleverest he he ever made, but it was devoted to ridiculing and answering a somewhat pompous oration made by the chairman for the evening, who was a very im-

portant local big-wig, and the corner-
stone of party organization in the district.
That was the last engagement he ever got
from either political party. Again and
again he would get something like regular
employment; now as a tutor, now on the
staff of a newspaper, but it always ended in
his returning to the library at the British
Museum, with empty pockets, and no fixed
work. A series of articles he had written
for a provincial paper on County Annals,
had made him think of writing about pedi-
gree and family history. Thanks to his
erudition and imagination, several gentlemen of large fortunes are at this moment
able to hang up a luxuriant family tree
in their smoking-rooms or libraries.

This pursuit lead to his finding his
way to the Record Office, and there
he had first heard and thought of the
funds in Chancery, and had begun to try
to make some use of his smattering of
law, in unearthing some treasure from
legal dust-heaps.

There were a good many others
engaged in the same pursuit,—people of
both sexes and all conditions; some
professionals, like Sam; others who
believed themselves to be personally
entitled to funds. Some of the latter
have grown old in the Record Office,

turning over musty pages, searching for
some document which they have taught
themselves to believe would complete their
case, and entitle them to a share of the
fund. If they left off the search, that
years since has become hopeless, they
would have nothing left to live for. A
bent, elderly man, a thin, grey-haired
woman, a young man, and a girl,
make up one family group. The elders
have grown grey, their children have
grown old, in the vain search. The
attendants know them as well as they
know the room itself, but do not know,
nor does any one else, what the fund
is to which they think they have a
claim ; or how they hope to prove it.
Father, mother, son and daughter, have
the same blurred look in the eyes, arising
from constant poring over the indices to
the names of suits. They must have
gone a hundred times over every name,
though there are huge bookcases full of
nothing but these indices. Now and then,
once a month or so, they will send for
some record, and they will seize with
wolfish glee upon the faded parchment
that the attendants bring them, and their
faces will light up with joy, and they will
spend days in deciphering and pondering
over the crabbed old writing, until the

hopeful looks fade away from their faces, and they go back to their endless hunt through the indices.

Among the professionals, there are spruce lawyer's clerks, who know exactly what they want, and where to get it, who hurry in, ask for their record, copy it, and go away again. There are others, who, like Sam, choose a case, and then hunt it up, on the chance of dragging something out of Chancery, and being paid salvage. Young and middle-aged women, who are paid, either by lawyers or antiquarians, to hunt up records, are at work there. One, a pretty girl, of perhaps twenty years, makes quite a good living by copying records. Her soft blue eyes having grown so familiar with the crabbed legal writing, that she can read off easily the work of even the most illegible of dead and gone clerks-in-chancery.

Sam Paradine sometimes looks at these young women, and thinks how hard it goes with girls who have to work for a living, and wonders how his sister Nelly likes being a governess.

For once in his life, Sam Paradine had been fairly lucky. The case of Smith *versus* Matterson appeared to be simple. At the end of the last century, Matterson, the husband of the defendant in the case, had died in debt. His estate in land had been administered by the Court of Chancery, on the petition of Smith, a creditor. There had been a surplus, after paying the debts, which was the fund in court. The case was clear, and what made matters more hopeful was that Sam had not found much difficulty in tracing at Somerset House the representatives of Matterson, down to a Mr. George Matterson of Brighton, who had died some thirty years before, leaving two daughters. The family appeared to have gone down in the world, for Mr. George Matterson described himself in his will as a " Licensed Victualler," and appeared to have been landlord of the Regent's Head, Brighton. " Those girls or their representatives, are entitled to the snug little fund of two thousand pounds," thought Samuel to himself, as he finished making his notes on the papers in the case, which seemed clear enough ; and ten per cent on two thousand pounds meant two hundred pounds, and that seemed very little for the man who had worked the whole thing up, to ask. Sam thereupon indulged in a splendid day-dream of what he could do if he only had two hundred pounds. He would go down into the country, and work steadily, and by the time he had spent the two hundred pounds, he would have earned more than that sum. But between him and the realization of that dream there were several obstacles. It entailed a journey to Brighton, and that would cost something. Sam fingered the few shillings in his pockets, which was all he had just then, and wouldn't be enough to take him down there. Then, as he walked away down Fetter Lane to Fleet Street, he caught sight of Tommy Rogers.

"We saw your thing is in 'The Bohemian.' Capital, every one says it is; congratulate you my dear old boy. Look here, old chap. You've only got to stick to it, and there's a big fortune before you. We shall have you living in a house across the park, and setting up your carriage before long. Why not? I say. Dash it all, that story of yours is better than anything Blank does, and he's making his two thousand a year.—Look here, old man; I s'pose you drew your cheque to-day. Now, like a good fellow, could you—"

"No, Sam, my boy, I drew it in advance, ever so long ago. All I got to-day was three numbers of the magazine, which I sold for fourpence each, and I've spent the shilling," answered Rogers. " I was going to ask you if you could—but I s'pose it is no good ? "

" Well, I'm blowed ! " said Sam, mournfully ; then he burst into a laugh as he thought of Bolster waiting outside the office of the magazine ; and he described to Tommy what would take place. " And what makes it so cruel is that I've a capital good thing on, if I could only raise a pound or so."

" Yes, it's hard luck. I daresay half the people who read that story of mine to-day will think what a clever chap the fellow who wrote it is, and what pots of money he must be making. And here I am ; by George ! but look here, Sam, I thought you were fairly flush by your looks. You have got 'em in your jaw still."

" By Jingo ! so I have. One gets so used to having 'em, that, believe me, I'd never have thought of it, if it hadn't been for you ; but it seems rather hard to have to pawn one's teeth in order to get a dinner, but they ain't much good if one hasn't anything to eat with 'em."

In his palmy days Sam had had his front teeth knocked out in a town and gown row. They had been replaced by a set of artificial ones which were set in gold. Several times before now, Sam had walked about for months with empty jaws. But as of late, pedigree-hunting had proved fairly remunerative, he had not found it necessary to part with them, and he had grown so accustomed to have them in his mouth again that he had forgotten all about them as an available asset.

It was a happy thought of the wily Tommy Rogers to remind him of it; so without any more words, Sam put his hand to his mouth, extracted the work of art-dentistry, and, with shrunken jaws, slipped round the corner and into the nearest pawnbroker's. Returning to his friend, they repaired to the shelter of a friendly public-house.

Sam now had enough funds to dine, get down to Brighton, and have a few shillings left for possible needs.

CHAPTER XX.

SAM STRIKES A REEF.

As he sat in a third-class carriage, bound for Brighton, with his toothless gums pressing against a black clay pipe, Sam Paradine indulged in a pleasant forecast of his future. His luck, at last, seemed to be turning. It might be rather difficult to find out anything about the children of Mr. George Matterson, of the Regent's Head, but the chances seemed in his favour. If he did find them, surely he might make a bargain that would be very much to his advantage. For years he had never had enough money in his pocket to enable him to look beyond the immediate future. As a rule he had never quite known where his next week's rent would come from. How he had lived at all was a mystery! But only make him secure and comfortable for a week or two, and he would turn out some good work, that would surprise every one!

Landed at Brighton, he felt a sense of

depression. After all, his quest might turn out a snare and disappointment.

It was with nervous hands that he turned over the pages of a Brighton directory, which he borrowed in a public-house; and he experienced a feeling of relief, when he found that the Regent's Head still existed. The appearance of the Regent's Head made him more hopeful. It was an old-fashioned, quiet-looking house, with none of the glitter of plate-glass of the modern gin-palace; and when he walked in he noticed that behind the bar there was a snug little parlour, in which there were old-fashioned pictures of coaching and racing scenes, and a stiff portrait of the member for Brighton of a by-gone age. The furniture and pictures in the parlour must have been pretty much the same in the Mattersons' time. It was just the place about which the memory of a former proprietor would cling and mellow in an atmosphere of hot grog and long clay pipes. There was an arm-chair, which he felt certain was occupied of an evening by some old fellow who had used the room for half a century, and probably had been godfather to one of the daughters of the George Matterson, deceased. Behind the bar was a buxom personage, fair, fat, and considerably over forty, whom Sam at once put down as the landlady. She brightened up when Sam made his inquiries.

"Know anything of the Mattersons?" Why, she could remember, like as if it were only yesterday, the day old Mr. Matterson died. She was a barmaid at the Regent's Head in those days, and afterwards had married the new landlord. She then went on to describe exactly where she was standing serving a gentleman with a hot brandy-and-water, when Sarah Matterson as was came up sudden to her, and told her that Mr. Matterson was gone.

"And the Misses Mattersons, do you happen to know where they are?" asked Sam, after he had let her thus run on.

"That, sir, I don't; leastwise Susan is in 'eaven, but Sarah I have never seen but once since she married, and that was just-by-chance-like in London, and mighty stuck-up and 'aughty she seemed to be, 'cause she'd married a gentleman. But for all that, not happy-looking, and if it came to changing places with 'er, for all 'er pride, I'd have said 'No thank yer.'"

"Sarah married?" said Sam, taking out his note-book, "To whom, and where was she married?"

" She was married at the old church round the corner, and she was married to a Captain Warleigh of the Lancers. An' very proud she was to catch a fine gentleman like that. It was quite a story, such as one reads about in a novel. The Captain, he quartered at the barracks here, and Sarah, after 'er father died, lost the little money that was left 'er, and came back to 'elp behind the bar; and I don't deny but what she brought custom, though perhaps not of the kind we wish. Well, once or twice when I was out with Sarah, we meets the Captain a-ridin' at the head of his soldiers, and she'd always talk about him, 'ow 'andsome he was, and 'ow like he was to parties she'd read about in her story-books—for she was a terrible gal to read. She always had it even then, that the 'andsome Captain a-ridin' at the 'ead of his troop, took particular notice of 'er, though I never paid no attention to 'er, and thought it all rubbidge. But sure enough, after the regiment went away, the Captain comes back agen, and 'eavy swell though he was, he comes to our place, day after day, a-drinkin' sherry wine and a-courtin' Sarah. I kept on telling 'er to mind what she was doing; and she says ' I know what I'm about,' and so she did, for it ended in his marryin' 'er, fair and honest, at St. James' Church round the corner, as I saw with my own eyes, and as you can see in the parish register, if you care to go and see it."

Sam seemed to remember the name Captain Warleigh, but it had no particular associations in his mind. Anyhow, his wife, or widow, if she were alive, would not be very hard to find. It would, he thought, be well worth while to have a look at the parish register. Mrs. Butun, the landlady of the Regent's Head, remembered the date of the wedding, by the date of the birth of her eldest son, a considerable proportion of whose infantine biography Sam was treated to, before he was allowed to leave in quest of the register. Having obtained access to it, he found the entry he was looking for without much difficulty.

"John Warleigh, second son of Sir George Warleigh, baronet, of Warleigh Park," was the name of the bridegroom.

When he left the vestry Sam went into a bookseller's shop and borrowed a "Baronetage." When he turned to the title Warleigh he gave a low whistle of astonishment. "It is my old luck," was his first thought. Sarah Matterson, who married John Warleigh, Captain of the

—th, would probably not be so easy to find after all, for in the "Baronetage" Captain John Warleigh, of that regiment, was stated to have married six months after the date of the entry he had just seen. It also stated that he married " Helen, daughter of the Rev. Percy Dalton, Rector of Saint Paul's, Fetchester."

" Looks rather fishy that," thought Sam to himself, as he remembered the landlady's story of having seen Sarah Matterson, who married Captain Warleigh, a year after his marriage. Rather an awkward business it looked for Captain Warleigh. Well, he was dead and gone, but how about Sir John Warleigh, present baronet, the son of the aforesaid Captain Warleigh, who had succeeded on the death of his cousin, the late Sir George Warleigh, and whom, Sam noticed, had been educated at Fetchester Grammar School? And how would the discovery affect Sam Paradine? Well, first of all it looked as if Sarah Matterson, who, by the register in St. James' Church, had become Mrs. Warleigh, would not be found very easily. The two hundred pounds he had settled upon, as the price for restoring the fund to its owners, seemed to fade away to nothing, and leave him *sans* teeth, *sans* everything except two or three odd shillings. On the other hand he was in possession of a secret that was undoubtedly worth money to some one.

"Cecil James, a captain in the Loyal Lancers, the youngest son of Sir George Warleigh, the sixth baronet," for instance, might be very much interested in that entry in the register of St. James' Church. Sam felt that his position was somewhat like that of a gold-digger, who has come across a rich quartz reef, which, though of great value, wanted capital to work it.

Going back to the Regent's Head, he made a few more inquiries about Sarah Matterson. The landlady was certain about the dates of the occasion when she had seen Sarah in London.

"I had been to London," she said, "for a day with Mrs. Crow of the Three Crowns, to a Licensed Victuallers' Fête, at the Crystal Palace, when, who should she come across—sudden-like—near Charing Cross, but Sarah Matterson as was. She didn't seem pleased to see us, and when I asked her how she got on with the Captain, she answered very short-like, and calls a cab, gets into it without asking after Butlin, nor the baby, as she 'ad often nursed, nor nothin'. And Mrs. Crow— a woman as I never liked, and don't acquaint with now—she says to me, ' Your old friend Sarah didn't want to have no more to do with you now—she is one of them as prosperity doesn't agree with.' If prosperity ailed Sarah, it's a sort of thing I don't want, for she looked worn and unhappy lookin', for all her pride ; though the Captain's lawful wife she was. A very haffable gent he was too, with manners as would take any woman. I remember once he asked me to change a cheque for ten pounds, which I did, and Butlin was in a rare way about it, a-sayin' ' as Captain ' or no Captain's, it was a thing we never did, but it come as ' right as rain ' as the sayin' is, an ' many a time have I thought of Sarah since, but never a word hev' I 'eard of her. The Captain was killed in the Rooshun War, I 'eard tell, but 'ow Sarah was left or whether she lived to be a widow or no, was what I never knewed."

Sam sucked his pipe and listened to the good woman rambling on, and later when he was travelling back to London, he pictured her in the witness-box giving evidence in a sensational ejectment case of Warleigh *versus* Warleigh ; in the issue of which he, Samuel Paradine would have a considerable stake.

CHAPTER XXI.

DISMAL JIMMY LAYS AGAINST "THE CRIER."

MR. KIT LUKES, like many another strong man, had his weaknesses, and one of them was a belief in the wisdom of going crooked on all occasions.

The most promising of speculations, if it happened also to be an honest one, would always lack a charm to him. It almost seemed he loved a robbery for its own sake. It was true that at fifty years old, he had managed to make a good deal of money, but then he had always been careful in his personal expenditure. He had no expensive tastes or vices, while on the other hand, he had good brains, which would have made his success in his profession a certainty, if he had worked at it in a more legitimate way. His start in life, too, had been a very fair one. The son of a country solicitor with a good old-fashioned practice, it seemed that his future was assured, and that he would in due time succeed to his father's place, and would find a splendid chance for making the very best of his abilities in increasing the family practice, and, in time, becoming one of those powerful lawyers who so quietly get their strong grip on to so much property, and become a power in the country.

If only the sort of honesty which is the best policy had come more easily to him, he would have probably been far better off than he was. But before he was thirty he had made his native town too hot for him.

Some very unpleasant revelations in the Probate Court, in a case about a disputed will, which it was proved he had persuaded an imbecile client to make in his favour, induced a good many of the older Lukes' most influential patrons to let him know that they would take their business away from the office, if young Christopher were not removed from it.

Before that scandal his reputation was none too good, owing to one or two coups he had made at race-meetings in the country, for Kit was a born sportsman, and very soon on entering man's estate became a sporting man. For a respectable country lawyer, he was a little too

clever, and lacked prudence in his un-
scrupulousness.

Old Lukes knew that young Kit had
the making of a very clever lawyer in him ;
but there was not much love lost between
the two, and there was another son to
take his place. So Kit got a place as
managing clerk to a London solicitor,
and, taking his own line, very soon found
himself cut adrift from his home people.

Many a man with a tithe of his
ability and not much less principle, had
become a respectable, prosperous London
lawyer.

But Kit could not keep his hands
out of the dirt, and very soon after he
started in business on his own account,
he got into the groove, which he always
afterwards kept in—that of a shady
bill-discounter and sharp practising at-
torney.

Sometimes, perhaps, it occurred to him,
that his life was not altogether a successful one, and he might doubt whether he
had not carried his maxim of "having
no infernal nonsense " in the way of a
scruple about him almost to an excess.
But after his return from his trip to Broxton
Down, he was thoroughly satisfied with
things in general. He saw an opportunity for bringing off the kind of coup

which had the strongest fascination for
him. For years there had not been so
much speculation on the Grand National.

The young men about town were,
almost to a man, anxious to have their
money on the horse that he knew could
have as scant a chance of winning as
if it were already scratched. All he had
to do was to consider how he could get
most out of the situation.

One day he was walking along the
Strand, his mind occupied with that
pleasant subject, when he ran into the
arms of an acquaintance,—of whom—
curiously enough—he was just thinking—
a tall gaunt man with a singularly
lugubrious expression of countenance,
which was remarkably in keeping with
his " get up : " he was attired as though
he had but just returned from assisting
at some funeral cortege.

" Well, Jimmy," said Mr. Lukes,
" you're just the man I want. How goes
it ? come round to my office."

" I've nothing to complain of Kit, so
far as making money is concerned ; but
I don't like the life I lead," answered the
melancholy man. " I don't feel comfortable in my mind about it, you see ;
say what you like, for a man of my turn
of thought, it isn't in keeping."

" Ah, yes, I take it, the elders or deacons, or whatever you call yourselves of that chapel at Ball's Pond, wouldn't altogether approve of Dismal Jimmy, if they knew him as we do."

" No, indeed they wouldn't, but they don't know. They think I am something in the Stock Exchange line. In fact, our pastor, who is speculating with his wife's fortune, came to me the other day, and asked, if I could tell him anything about gold shares. I should be shunned like a pauper, if they thought I was a betting-man."

" Ay, Dismal Jimmy or the Under-taker, who is said to have worked more commissions against ' dead 'uns,' than any one else in the ring, would not be considered quite respectable by the par-son who gambles in Wild Cat Mining Companies."

" Yes, and the question is, Mr. Lukes, can betting be right ? I doubt it. All the associations of the business are revolting to me. If ever there was a convinced Good Templar, I am one, and one has to meet a class of company, which, say what you will, Mr. Lukes, isn't desirable or im-proving."

" Why don't you drop it, then ? " asked Mr. Lukes, as they turned the corner of a street off the Strand, where he carried on his business.

" A wife and six children make it hard for a man to give up a good living.   I have never found anything else at which I seemed to have the slightest turn of luck.   I went in for publishing a religious newspaper, but bless you, a man who has cut his teeth in the betting ring ain't in it, with the lot in that line.   I dropped in my money and got fleeced. I've been in the wholesale treacle line, in a Heathen Clothing Company—you know the line—six per cent. dividends in this world with a biblical prospectus—but I never could do any good, the lot are so artful, that I couldn't last with 'em, and had to turn betting-man again."

" And a pretty good thing you make of it, don't you, Jimmy, my boy ?   And now to business.   I want you to work a commission for me, on the Grand National. How much can you lay against ' The Crier ' ? "

" The Crier ! why, they're all mad to back it !   The swells won't touch anything else, except Lord Bamborough's horse."

" Then lay all you can against it for me.   Lay to lose fifty thousands, but get every penny there is in the market to go on the Crier."

"Dear, dear, so the Crier is to be made a dead 'un of—to use the revolting language of the ring. Well, that is sad, for all the young men are wild to back it. Still, it will be a useful lesson for them, Mr. Lukes, better in the end for them to lose their money than to win it, for say what you will, betting is an unhealthy occupation. In fact, I am very much inclined to put it down as absolutely wrong. Let us hope that if the Crier has been made a ' stiff 'un,' it may teach a very useful lesson to many a young man, and Mr. Lukes, you may depend upon my getting pretty nearly all there is to be got out of it."

" Well, Jimmy, I'm always game to read 'em that sort of lesson, I have shown 'em once or twice the folly of backing favourites, but ' a fool is born everysecond,' thank goodness," said Kit, and the two parted.

That conversation accounted for a fact which was much commented upon in the sporting papers, namely, that though there seemed to be an enormous sum of money in the market to back the Crier, the horse was persistently opposed in a very dangerous quarter.

Dismal Jimmy's mournful voice was always heard declaring his willingness to lay against the Crier.

On the other hand, among a certain class of young men, it become almost an article of faith that backing the Crier was a certain cure for impecuniosity.

It was the best thing there had been for years, and his victory was simply a matter of whether he kept on his legs.

Cecil Warleigh's luck seemed to turn. He rode in a good many races about that time, and nearly always won. The Grand Military Steeple-chases at Sandown that year were a particularly bright and successful reunion. Cecil was to ride in the Grand Military a horse that belonged to Lord Lomond, a brother officer, and the gallant Loyal Lancers. were to a man standing to win their money on his mount. Cecil had won two other races, on horses that Jack had given him, and which were trained by Tom Ring.

" We're in rare form just now, Captain," said honest Tom, his good-looking face all aglow and wreathed in smiles, when Cecil had weighed in after the second of these races, " I didn't feel over confident about to-day, but the Liverpool race has never looked such a sure thing ; " and the trainer's words were known all over the course in a very short time, and soldiers of all ranks and corps had their money on the Crier for Liverpool.

Many a gallant officer's name was written in Jimmy Grueby's book, and still his raven-like voice was lifted up offering to bet on 'the field.' All was fish that came to his net, he would lay the odds to hundreds, or to a few sovereigns as the backer required.

"Five to two on the field, for the Grand National," he chanted out, as if he were foretelling the doom of the human race, but still undefeated and undaunted.

Men who knew most about the betting-ring, shrugged their shoulders when they heard the refrain, and wondered what was wrong.

"Don't like that carcass-merchant's way of going on," said Sir Peregrine Evergreen, a veteran of the turf, who had seen his own colours beaten for the last time, some twenty years before, but still went from race-course to race-course, investing his fivers with a good deal more discretion than he did his 'monkeys' in the days of his prosperity, to Captain Baxter, late of the ——th regiment, who owning a good pair of eyes, a sharp pair of ears, and unruffled prudence, found that backing horses was better than going on the Stock Exchange or Mark Lane, as some of his retired brother-in-arms had done ; and being swindled, as they were, by City sharpers.

" He has overlaid any possible book he can have made, but I fancy he doesn't make much of a book ; looks as if he were at his old business and betting on commission," answered Captain Baxter. " He has laid for Kit Lukes before now."

" What, is Lukes backing, then ? " asked Sir Peregrine. " I think he is the more dangerous man of the two."

" I saw him take the odds to a ' pony ' about Jack Sheppard on Friday, at Kempton. There are some people who say that he thinks that he is sure to win with that," answered the Captain.

" Never found Kit Lukes let a dozen men hear him back a horse of his, when he really did feel sweet about it."

" Ah, if Mr. Jimmy Grueby told all he knew about Kit Lukes, that gentleman would find that there was not room enough for him on Newmarket Heath."

" They say Kit never trusts a man, unless he knows enough about him to send him to penal servitude," replied the Captain.

" Kit is an infernal scoundrel," remarked Sir Peregrine, " and has done enough to have a thousand men warned off. I wish to goodness I knew what his game is for Liverpool, though—there go up the numbers for the next race. The Military Heavy Weight Handicap ; what do you fancy for it ? "

" I hear," answered the Captain, " that Wide-awake, owned by Mr. Jones of the ' Worzelshire Light Infantry,' is being backed. No. 5, Lord Lomond's Ajax with Cecil Warleigh up, is the favourite, they always back Warleigh's mount at this meeting. I shall back Wide-awake, off the course ; he won't be backed for a penny here. I shall have ' a pony ' on him."

" I'll have a tenner on, that's a big sum for me," said Sir Peregrine, and they both turned away to the telegraph.

The saddling bell for the next race was ringing as, after sending off their messages, they hurried to the paddock where horses were being stripped, and knots of admirers were gazing at the starters for the Handicap.

CHAPTER XXII.

THE GRAND MILITARY.

THE horses engaged in the Grand Military were this year decidedly above the average class. The Household Brigade contributed some half-dozen candidates, the most fancied of them being Sailor Boy, owned by Lord Lutterworth, of the Royal Horse Guards, and ridden by his owner, who was, perhaps, more in his element following the Quorn than between the flags; but for all that, bad to beat anywhere : a splendid horseman, and the hardest of hard riders.

The Royal Horse Artillery, that most sporting of corps, had as usual a likely candidate. On Captain Jubber's Curragh Wren the hopes of Woolwich were centred, the mare having carried all before her at their meeting at Eltham some weeks before, and the gunners had backed her to a man. But they feared Ajax, Cecil Warleigh's mount, which starts a strong favourite.

"That fellow looks more like riding in a Farmer's Stakes than in the Grand Military," says Sir Peregrine to Captain Baxter, pointing to a young man, whose large, red face was set off by a yellow silk cap. He had an old brown country-made great-coat, such as young rustics wear on a Sunday, buttoned over his racing jacket, and altogether looked like anything but an officer in the army. An old, hard-bitten looking groom was holding his horse.

"Yes, he doesn't look very smart, but I fancy he can ride," replied Captain Baxter. "I like the look of the mare Wide-awake as well as any of them ; and the lot behind Mr. Jones of the Wurzle-shire regiment are clever enough. His uncle is Bill Jones who trains up Northallerton way—and Wide-awake was a goodish mare at the flat two years ago, but a little slow."

Sir Peregrine thought it seemed a good thing to back the horse, as his friend went on to tell him how he had smelt a rat on seeing Mr. Jones, Senior, the father of the sulbaltern of the Wurzleshire regiment, busy taking the long odds ; and had got the information from him, that they intended to get up a little surprise for the army.

Mr. Jones, Senior, who was whispering

a few last words to his son, was an elderly
man, dressed like a dissenting grazier in
a greasy black suit of clothes, the pockets
of which bagged out as if he were carrying his things for the night in them,
which, as a matter of fact, was the
case.

"There's enow brass on t'ould mare to
pay for cramming thee for t' army, and
there's nowt to fear but Warleigh, an'
thou'rt a bit better than him. We get a
foin price, I war'ant there's no one
backing t' mare, but that sly devil
Baxter who saw me, an' no doubt he told
ould Sir Peregrine, but they'll keep their
mouths shut, an' they do'ant plunge, for
they ain't got much t' lose. Did'st tell
any o' thy brother officers, lad?"

"Nay, father, they're a stook up lot,
and said I warn't bringing credit on th'
regiment, in making a fool o' myself in
public; they're a lot o' men as just know
nowt," said the youngster, as he pulled
off the great coat and displayed his
colours, a green jacket with yellow cap.

Young Jones was not a favourite in
the Wurzleshire regiment, who were a
peculiarly slow and sedate lot of men,
but were startled out of their usual
apathy by his curious pronunciation of
the Queen's English, his manner of

eating, and demeaning himself at mess, to say nothing of the general rusticity, not to say vulgarity, of his manners. He seemed very stupid about his drill and his duty, so much so, that he was believed to be a little deficient in intellect, and the notion of his having entered a horse for the Grand Military was considered a joke, which would have been a very excellent one, if it did not tend, to a certain extent, to throw ridicule on the regiment.

Jack Warleigh had come down to Sandown with the Cottinghams. For some little time he had felt puzzled at Kate's manner. They were excellent friends, and Jack was more in love with her than ever, yet she managed to prevent matters coming to a crisis. It seemed almost as if she had some sympathetic power over him that kept him from making the declaration she did not care to hear.

For the first time he felt half jealous of Cecil, and noticed what a thorough understanding there seemed to be between him and Kate.

" I am sure to win this race ; the other two I am doubtful about, but I can't be beaten this time," Cecil had said to her, just before the Grand Military. " This

is the first time I have backed my
mount. You had better follow my example."

"I always mistrust you when you're so
certain," Kate had answered. "In your
case it is the *unexpected* disaster that
always happens to upset your plans."

"You used to bring me luck, when you
watched me riding," Cecil answered; "it
ought to be the same now."

"The charm is broken, it seems, for
you had very little luck at Fetchester,
but we won't be out of spirits about it;
I am just the same in wishing you luck."

There was something in the tone of
her voice and in the look in her eyes
which startled Jack with the idea which
had never come into his mind before.
He recalled all the occasions on which he
had seen them together. The first
they had not met for some years, and
yet their greeting was cold and con-
strained. "Were they like two lovers
then?" he asked himself; but the unpleasant answer forced itself upon his
mind, that they were not unlike lovers
who had quarrelled. If there had been
nothing between them, why were they
not on better terms?

"I suppose you have seen Cecil ride a
great many races?" he said, somewhat

glumly, as he noticed the flash of excite-ment in her face as she watched his uncle on Ajax going down to the start.

"Oh, yes; a great many times, and I do hope he will win this race. I want to see our regiment beat the Guards and the Artillery. Don't you?" .

Of course he did. "What a brute he had been to object to her enthusiasm!" Jack declared to himself, and his good temper soon returned.

Cecil Warleigh had noticed Mr. Jones' Wide-awake, and had formed a favour-able impression of both horse and rider.

They made Ajax rather a hot favourite, taking a hundred to sixty about it. Curragh Wren and Sailor Boy being backed at three to one; a point or two more was laid against two or three of the other candidates; Wide-awake's price was a hundred to eight. Here and there it was quietly taken, once by Captain Baxter.

"Ajax looks as well as anything," remarked General Cottingham to his daughter, as the horses pass the Stand for the first time. Kate says nothing, but watches Lord Lutterworth, of whom she is most afraid.

A gallant rifleman leads, but it is obvious that his horse is out of condition; Sailor Boy is second, while Ajax and Curragh Wren lie behind with Wide-awake some length or so in their wake.

Two have already come to grief at the brook, two others are hanging out signals of distress.

"That fellow can ride right enough," says Captain Baxter to Sir Peregrine, as he looks approvingly at Wide-awake.

After negotiating a couple more fences, the hopes of the Rifle Brigade are snuffed out. The others keep their places.

A mile from home, it looked any one's race. The men of the Blues, Artillery and Lancers, all hope to secure the Soldier's Blue Ribbon.

"Jubber wins! we shall have the cup on the mess table at Woolwich, and nowhere else will it look so well," says a young gunner, who had just passed out of the Academy.

For a moment or so, it looks as if Sailor Boy will win, but Lutterworth has ridden his horse quite out, for he goes down at the last fence. Then comes a cry of "The favourite wins!" as Ajax passes Curragh Wren, who also gives place to Wide-awake. Ajax clearing the last fence, comes into the last field with a lead of two lengths.

"Ajax wins! Ajax wins!" is shouted by stentorian voices from the Grand Stand, and the Lancers think they have won their money. Captain Baxter, as he takes in the race, thinks differently.

"No, it's a race! The grey wins—here, what's this? Wide-awake wins! No, Ajax wins!" but the supporters of the latter are doomed to be disappointed.

Cecil Warleigh's horse has shot his bolt, and notwithstanding a bit of desperate riding on his part, Wide-awake passes him, full of running, and wins the Grand Military Gold Cup for the Wurzleshire regiment, easily enough, by two lengths.

"Who is he?"

"Jones—Wurzleshire regiment."

"That's the old —th, isn't it?"

"He won that race very cleverly?"

"What an infernal sell! Never heard of the confounded horse."

"Did pretty well on the flat, though, the season before last," says Baxter, consolingly, to a young guardsman, who seemed to be flabbergasted that a man in the Wurzleshire regiment should have beaten them all.

"Yes, I backed it, thought it a good thing."

When the race of the day is over, book-makers turn their attention to future events.

Mr. Grueby's voice is heard offering to lay against the Crier for the Grand National.

" What's wrong with the Crier ? " asked Lord Dargle of Jack Warleigh, " that fellow's opposition is generally rather sickly," he added, as Grueby's monotonous chant continued.

" Then he knows something that I don't know, that Cecil doesn't know, and Tom Ring doesn't know; for we three are all perfectly confident, and the horse is fit and well," replied Jack, turning to Grueby and asking,—

" What price do you say the Crier ? "

" A hundred to forty ! A thousand to five hundred ! Ten thousand to four thousand ! if you really want to back it, Sir John."

Jack had heard several whispers about the persistent opposition to the Crier, and he felt somewhat sore at the way the class of small speculators—who are always ready to invent a cock-and-bull story about an owner—shrugged their shoulders, and said that the stable had been forestalled, and were going to scratch the horse after they had got a lot of money out of him.

"I will take ten to four in thousands," said Jack, as he pulled out his book.

Mr. Grueby shook his head sadly, and entered the bet, and then there came a shoal of smaller backers, who followed the owner's money.

Mr. Grueby offered half-a-point less, but he still seemed willing to go on laying against the Crier.

"Keep your eyes wide open down at Warleigh, for I don't altogether like the look of Dismal Jimmy," said Lord Dargle to Jack, as they walked away.

"There's no fear, I tell you. Tom Ring, the trainer, is as honest as the day," answered Jack, "I'd as soon mistrust myself or Cecil as Tom Ring."

"It seems to be fated that you never win when you are certain," Kate whispered to Cecil, when he came up after the race for the Cup. "Will another of your plans be upset at Liverpool?"

"No, Liverpool is a certainty, that can't be upset."

"Not in a steeple-chase? Is the Crier sure to win?" she asked in a somewhat doubting tone, for she more than suspected the truth.

"No, to lose," replied Cecil, looking into her face, to see if the knowledge of what he was going to do made her feel repulsion. "I suppose it's nonsense for me not to be candid with you?"

"And you risk this for me, Cecil? It would be horrible for you if you were found out," she answered; but her face softened and a look that Cecil knew well enough came into her eyes. "Once it seemed that you would never care as much as that for me!"

CHAPTER XXIII.

SAM PARADINE DINES.

" SAMUEL, dear boy, I have a bit of luck," said Tommy Rodgers, the celebrated author, bursting into Sam Paradine's bedroom, on the morning after the latter's trip to Brighton—" and I want you to lend me a bob or two, and share it with me."

Sam Paradine had woke up on hearing the first part of the speech, and sat up in his bed, but he threw himself back again ; and, more or less, like a door on its hinges, he turned in his bed, and became dull and drowsy.

" I can't do it, old chap," he muttered in a somnolent voice, and, with a determined pull at the bed-clothes, he settled himself for sleep again.

" Hang it Sam, you ain't going to sleep again. It's quite late, you know—eleven o'clock—long past time to get up," said Mr. Rodgers, in the brisk manner of one who'd conquered sloth.

"But I don't mean to get up, I shall stay in bed till things mend a bit. Hard-up-ishness is an illness which I believe in lying up for."

"But, hang it, things won't mend while you stop in bed, on a beautiful morning like this," and Rodgers opened the window, and let the fog in, "get up, face the world like a man."

"Not me. When I am up, I am done. My landlady will catch me on the stairs, and if I don't pay her, she'll take the door off the latch when I go out, and not let me in again. No, I'm better in bed, besides, I want to think. Before Paley turned over a new leaf in his life and became an altered man, he stopped in bed, almost all day, thinking of himself and his future. Now, I have a lot to think over too, a very big thing that ought to make my future."

"And what plan can you think out in bed in a frowsy garret, with nothing to eat? No, sir, that is not the way to stimulate genius. If you want to think, have a good varied dinner of several courses, a bottle of dry champagne, and order a cup of coffee, a liqueur of brandy and a capital cigar, and as you smoke, if you don't find your ideas coming to you quickly and strongly, they never will come."

"Don't! don't, old chap! else I shall dream of it, and it is so beastly, waking up—but you're right, that is the way to think anything out, but if I had the means to get that sort of dinner, I should not bother about making plans."

"Get up, man, and dress. You shall have just that sort of dinner to-night. What do you say to a five-shilling dinner at the Paragon, with drinks in keeping? and to such a banquet I have got an invitation, and, what is more, I am asked to bring a friend. Ah! you wonder what the talisman was that procured it. It was the story, my boy, that I contributed to Gripps' confounded magazine."

"Your story! Why, has the proprietor of the Paragon taken to dining such representatives of literature as are going to be celebrated some day or other? Are you going to be entertained by a grateful public?"

"I daresay you did not notice that one of the best drawn characters in that brightly written narrative—Lord Edward—the unprincipled aristocrat, whose gluttony is neatly made a point of, always indulges in the five-shilling dinner at the Paragon. He has no less than

three of those dinners, in ten pages; well,
I went to see the proprietor there, this
morning. I knew him well enough in the
old days. Look at this, I said, and got
him to read the story. I believe an
author never pleased a man more than I
did that fellow. He said, ' It was capital,
a grand story.' "

" When I told him that I used to give
dinners at the Paragon, before I got broke
and took to literature, he answered with
enthusiasm that ' it would have been
a pity that any one who could write like
I did, should not have taken to it. But
I tell you what it is,' he said. ' You
shall dine here again; there will be a
table for you any night you like, and you
shall see that the lord you write about
was not wrong when he came to our five
bob ' set out.' It will be a table for four,
and you can bring some other literary
gents to dine with you; there'll be two
bottles of champagne, a bottle of port,
and a pint of sherry.' So, Sam, my boy, I
thought of you and I accepted. A glass of
sherry with your soup, a bottle of champagne with your dinner, and a half
bottle of port to wind up with : that's
the receipt for thinking. Plain living
and high thinking be hanged. With a
dinner like that inside you, you could

face a regiment of London landladies, all asking to be paid small accounts. But, have you a bob or two ? "

" Don't see what you want 'em for ? " said Sam, whose face had brightened up wonderfully during his friend's recital.

" Well, my boy, we want breakfast ; just a snack, you know. Such a dinner in prospect demands a breakfast, and I don't mind owning, that yesterday I forgot all about breakfast, thinking about the dinner, and spent all I had. Then, there's the waiter. A feast is spoiled when you see in the waiter's eye a look of mistrust as to whether he will get anything for himself or not, and you feel all the time that his mistrust is well-founded. Then again, that tie and collar of mine ain't what they ought to be. My clothes are all right, they're one of Blog's ' two guinea suits.' It was at Blog's, you'll remember, ' that the long-lost heir ' got his rig out. But my tie and collar are very weak. The infernal editor chucked the thing in which I gave the haberdasher a turn."

Sam Paradine had some three shillings left, and he handed his friend half of it.

" That's all right, that will do splendidly. A shilling for the waiter, and the modest sum of sixpence judiciously expended for the purpose of procuring a paper collar and some arrangement in the scarf line, and I shall be fit to walk in the Park. My hat is all right.—You remember my account of the returned Prodigal, 'And shabby though his garments were, they bore signs of having once been the pride of a West End tailor; while there was still that mark of workmanship about his tattered, caved-in hat, which clings to one of Brown's productions, even when it does duty on a scare-crow.' That was good for a decent tile."

" Does Gripps know of it ? " asked Sam.

" No, thank goodness ! he has never twigged. You see, he doesn't read his own magazine. In fact, I don't know that he can read."

" I suppose he'd stop it, if he did," asked Sam, " and say it lowered the dignity of his blessed periodical ? "

" Stop it, bless me, no, but he'd take care to get the plunder for himself."

Tommy Rogers, happy in the possession of the eighteen-pence that Sam had parted with, took his departure, previously mentioning the hour of six o'clock as being the hour at which the famous Paragon five-shilling dinner was served.

A good dinner is thrice-blessed. Good

to look forward to, doubly good to enjoy, and good to look back upon.

Sam thought little of his troubles and much of the coming feast. He was going to *dine*—not merely to get something to eat in a cheap and greasy cookshop. A feast of reason and a flow of soul is all very well in its way, but it was a poor thing, so he thought, when, day after day, it was enjoyed, unaccompanied by unattractive viands. He felt serenely happy, and when the landlady caught him on the stairs as he anticipated, and told him not to come back unless he brought his rent with him, he bore her tirade, to use Doctor Johnson's fine figure, "like a monument." He spent the day—it was one of those rare sunny days of early spring—in blissfully thinking of his evening's entertainment.

At the appointed hour he was waiting near the door of the Paragon for his talented friend. The very notion of dining again in an ample manner had given a certain dignity to Sam's gait and appearance. He had not dined there for the last twelve years, and then he was one of a jovial party of Christ Church men, three of whom were now English Peers, and the fourth Sam had met only a week or two before, acting as billiard marker at a third rate public-house. They had smoked several pipes together, drank a glass of gin and water, and had a long talk over old times. Yes, they had jovial times when he was sowing that large crop of wild oats that had sprung up so disastrously.

The arrival of Mr. Rogers, looking smart in an arrangement of white scarf and paper collar, checked Sam's thoughts of the past.

"I was thinking over old times, Tommy, when I used to dine here before; and, how different they were," he said, as the other joined him.

" Different, be blowed! ain't we going to have the five-shilling dinner, and as much as we can drink? Old days have come back again, for the time being," answered Rogers.

"I dined with Bamborough, Lomond, Haggis and Freddy Dormer, who was considered the handsomest man at Oxford, and who is now the marker at the Old Lark Pie."

" Hope everything is comfortable, gentlemen? Glad to see you here again, Mister. I remember your face very well, though I've not had the pleasure of seeing you for a long time. Have you took up literature too, sir? Well, gentlemen, I ain't one of them as despises literature. What

I says, is, literature ought to be the ' 'and-maid of commerce,' said the proprietor, coming to where they sat. "Now, if either of you gents could set that sentiment into print, as something I said, and work in a little about my five-shilling dinner into the same paragraph, why, I should be very happy to see both of you here again."

The dinner served to Tom Rogers and Sam Paradine was an excellent one.

" Well, it's years since I had a bottle of champagne," said Sam, when a second bottle was finished.

" He is a fine, liberal, large-hearted man, is Biffin, I'd like to write a three-volume novel, all about the place, and the dinners," said Tommy Rogers, as he sipped his glass of port. " The waiter looks like a character, one might bring him in, and the cook ; I'd like to bring 'em all in. Sammy, my boy, you've deserted literature—and for what ? Why, for fooling in that Record Office, where you'll never do any good. Fine sentiment, that of Biffins, ' Literature, the handmaid of Commerce,'—and yet you have deserted literature to grub among old papers, and become a drudge of the law."

By the time the wine was finished, the two friends had reached the argumentative stage, and they were discussing each other's positions in life, with a fatal candour.

"Let me tell you that a g'ologist—I mean a gene—al—lo—lol—olgist, holds a far better position than a penny-a-liner, and he finds out some very 'portant things, now an' then," stammered Sam.

"'Portant things! St-huff an' non-sense! where have you ever found out anything but bogus pedigrees for retired tradesmen?" answered Tommy Rogers, laughing, and somewhat unpleasantly, as he tossed off the remainder of his coffee and brandy.

"So you think; just listen to this, and then tell me I never find out any-thing," retorted Sam, and then at great length, he told, with much harking back and considerable circumlocution, the story of what he had found out at Brighton.

It was told in a very thick voice, which had perhaps a soothing effect; and when at last he had come to a conclusion, and demanded triumphantly of Tommy Rogers, "What he tho' o' that?" the latter was leaning with his elbow on the table, asleep.

For all that, however, Sam's eloquence had not been wasted. To the latter part of the story there had been one very attentive listener. A fresh-complexioned, middle-aged gentleman, who sat at the next table, had been inclined at first to feel annoyed with Sam Paradine's story. After he had finished his dinner, he had pulled out of his pocket what looked like a betting-book, and had become absorbed in some calculations, which were considerably disturbed by the noise his neighbours were making, and at first seemed inclined to remonstrate. After a little while a name caught his ear, which caused him to lean forward and listen eagerly to the rest of the story. When it was concluded, he got up and walked to the next table.

Touching Sam on the shoulder, he said :

" Excuse me, sir, but, do you think that bawling out a story like the one you've just told in a public dining-room, is quite prudent? I happen to know something about the family whose name you have been making so free."

Sam looked somewhat aghast at the stranger, who stared him out of countenance, with a pair of cunning little blue eyes.

" Now, if you take my advice, sir, you'll give me your name and address, and call on me to-morrow morning, when we can have a little talk about the matter. My name is Christopher Lukes, solicitor, 10,

Burleigh Street, Strand ; I shall be in to-morrow morning at 11.30.

"Shan't call on you. Know your infernal place, been there once too often, as it is, Mr. Kit Lukes," answered Sam.

"Ah, I thought somehow we had met before. Now I remember you. Mr. Samuel Paradine, of Christ Church, Oxford. You and Mr. Dormer borrowed fifty pounds from me, on a bill, and you both went bankrupt, and I never got paid a penny. But that is past and gone, I don't bear any malice ; but take my advice, call on me to-morrow, and to begin with, you had better let me have your present address. Believe me, if there is anything in this story, which you have told this gentleman, who doesn't appear to be very interested in it, you will want some one at your elbow, who knows how to look after you. A secret may be valuable so long as it is a secret, but it isn't worth much if it is bellowed out by a drunken man. As it is, I know about as much as you do, if there's anything in the story you've just told.

Sam felt a good deal more sober than he had done a moment or so before. His friend's prescription for stimulating the mind had been a little overdone, but there was no need for him to regret that, as it was pretty clear that Mr. Kit Lukes would save him the trouble of having to think out the matter, as he evidently intended to take the management into his own hands. Still, Sam did not feel himself strong enough to contend against the lawyer, whose masterful manner at once gained an ascendency over him.

"Don't know about my address," said Sam. "I left my lodgings to-day, and I was going to get my friend to give me a shake down."

"Come along with me, then, you can sleep at my office, and then you will be there the first thing in the morning, when I shall want to talk to you," said Mr. Lukes. And so satisfied was he with the cheap rate at which he saw he was going to acquire information that he thought might become valuable, that he went out of his way to give Mr. Rogers a lift home, and then drove round to his office, where he deposited Sam Paradine, who was content enough to pass the night on a horse-hair sofa, with a railway rug thrown over him. It was better than wandering about the streets, which had seemed by no means an improbable finish to an evening which had begun with an expensive dinner.

Sam found himself a mere child in the hands of the lawyer.

" Before you sell information, you will have to learn to keep your mouth shut, and not give it away. As it is, I know almost as much as I want to," was the way in which Mr. Lukes put it to him the next morning, when he called at an early hour at the office. Sam thought to himself that it was all the port after the champagne. " But, for all that," Mr. Lukes said, with an air of magnanimity, " he was determined to give Sam a turn. He wanted some one to look up the case, and Sam might as well do it as any one else ; and if the case became important, Sam would have a good present made to him."

After expressing himself thus, he sat down and wrote several letters. One was to a money-lender, who he believed would have in his possession several letters written by the late Captain Warleigh, asking for specimens of handwriting. Another was to an expert in whose opinion he had some little confidence.

" You'll have to accompany the gentleman to whom you will hand this letter, down to Brighton, and show him the entry in the register ; and whatever you do, don't talk. Last night ought to be a lesson to you for life," said Mr. Lukes, giving Sam the letter, and a great many directions as to how he should work up the case, together with a few pounds for expenses. He then left the office. He had plenty to do just then; for it was but a few days before the Grand National; and he did not, to tell the truth, believe very much in Sam Paradine's discovery, but Lukes was a man who never missed a chance.

Sam's golden dreams had turned to a very commonplace reality. Still he found himself with a little ready-money; and those acquainted with his financial barometer must have known that his funds had risen considerably, for a fine set of glistening teeth once more adorned his gums.

CHAPTER XXIV.

AT LIVERPOOL.

"I am full against it, sir; can't lay the Crier any more," said Jimmy Grueby to Lord Dargle, who had come up to him in the big billiard room of the Washington Hotel, on the evening before the Grand National.

"Hear that?" said keen-eyed Captain Baxter, nudging the arm of his friend, Sir Peregrine.

"Looks more healthy; I believe the horse will start a terribly short price," answered the baronet, who noticed how men were whispering together, and looking at the book-maker, who for weeks had been the arch enemy of the favourite, but who now seemed to own that he had done enough.

Lord Dargle went to another book-maker, and was offered five to two to a small amount. The horse had gone up a point in the betting, and at a shortened price was backed very generally, while most of the layers seemed to fight very shy of betting more than a small sum against the horse.

"Isn't there one of you here who will lay me the odds to a monkey?" said Dargle. "Well, you are a poor lot."

"I think I can manage it for you, my lord, as the professionals seem to· be afraid to do any real business," said a fresh-complexioned gentleman, who was sitting near Jimmy Grueby. "You know me, I think, my lord—Lukes—Christopher Lukes, of Burleigh Street."

"And a very hard lot too, is Mr. Kit Lukes," whispered Captain Baxter to his friend. "As soon as one battery is silenced another opens fire. My opinion is that those two are working in concert."

"Well, Burke, what have you done about to-morrow?" asked Sir Peregrine of Major Burke, who stopped to say a word as he was leaving the room.

"The favourite. I don't like taking such a short price, but it can't be helped," answered Dick Burke. "Cecil Warleigh, who backed the horse at longer odds— lucky beggar—laid me twelve to four in hundreds."

"Oh, Warleigh backed it at long odds, did he?" said Baxter. "Well, he can keep it all to himself as far as I am concerned, I'm not sure I like the way its going on in the market. Don't like so much opposition from that quarter," and Baxter nodded his head in the direction in which Lukes was standing. The latter gentleman had laid several other bets against the Crier, and still offered to go on.

"Oh, it's all right. There would be the deuce to pay if there was anything wrong. Dargle has backed the horse for a lot of money, and when he is hard hit, he is determined to purify the turf of those who have got six to four the best of him."

"I don't say there is anything wrong, mind you. All I do say is, that I don't care about it at the price. It ain't the certainty men think it to be. There are several pretty good ones in the race this year, reminds me of old times. There's that horse of Bamborough's—Middy—he has a big chance, so they tell me, and I like his looks well enough, and what I have seen of him—he ran third last year, and if he is as much improved as people say, he ought to come very near winning at the weights. I should back him if Bamborough would not ride. By the way, Major, what about the Irish lot?"

"Faith, I know nothing about 'em. Life is not long enough for one to try and see what games that lot won't be up to. Napper Tandy is their best, but it's three years since he won the race, and doesn't grow any younger, an' may-be he isn't meant," said the Major, as he nodded "Good night," and left the room.

Baxter smoked his cigar and came to the conclusion that the best thing he could do would be to leave it alone. His own judgment seemed to point clearly enough to the favourite, while there were several others he had heard a great deal about. There was the Limpet, fancied by an extremely clever division who trained at Epsom ; Master Dick, the hope of the Cheltenham people ; Paladin, who had won several steeple-chases in France, and a Hungarian horse—Ulda— who had carried all before it in Germany. These represented the Continental opposition ; and both were undoubtedly dangerous. Then there was Jack Sheppard, who was an honest horse enough, and of the twenty who would probably face the starter, there were some half-a-dozen others who had been lately backed for a good bit of money. The field was not a weak one.

"But there's nothing to touch the Crier," Captain Baxter said, "only I would like to know what Kit Lukes has to go on."

On the day of the Grand National there was a cold white mist spread over the country. Just the sort of weather to give a man the "blues," and make him feel nervous and out of heart, Cecil Warleigh thought, as, muffled in a long great coat and a wrapper, he walked nervously about the paddock, and tried to dodge away from the many old friends who kept pestering him about the race. It was curious. what a lot of men whom he had not seen for a long time; good fellows whom he liked, and whom he hated to think he was helping to rob. He was not like some men, who positively revel in a robbery, and greatly enjoy winning their money by foul means, more than by fair. Pat Considine, for instance, would have been in capital spirits if he had only been cast for his part. "Well, thank goodness! the mist will be all in my favour, they may think what they like, but the most malicious of them won't be able to see much," he thought, as he stood on the Grand Stand and looked through the mist down the course.

"Hallo, old boy, wish you luck. I have

a pony on your mount, for the sake of old times. I thought I'd manage to get to Liverpool once more to see you win, though times are rather hard just now," said a cheery, hearty voice, and Gordon, late of his regiment, an old comrade with whom he'd never had a bad word during the ten years they were in the regiment together, gave his hand a hearty grip.

"They tell me that the regiment are all on, and that there will be great times when you have pulled off the race."

Cecil mumbled out a few words in reply, and bustled away. He ought to have realized before, how hateful it would be to go wrong.

But there was no time for repentance. He must be true to Kit Lukes and company, and let in all his old friends. He hardly saw the first two races, and he never spent a worse hour.

Before the first race, he caught sight of a face he once knew well enough, Jack Flamby, who in old days was his rival, a rider in military races. He was in the crowd outside the enclosure, struggling to get up to an ill-looking list-man, to invest the few shillings he had managed to borrow from some old comrade of his palmy days.

"Hang the fellow, how the devil does

he manage to get here?   I wish to goodness he had stopped away for once," Cecil said to himself, as he turned away from the once popular, dashing, and cheery dragoon. But he could not get that face out of his mind.   How coarse and shameless the man had become, with his half-defiant, half-cringing demand for alms in the guise of a loan.   And to remember that it was only three years since his fall.   Cecil felt himself shivering, how he wished he was out of it all.   What a fool he had been to bet against his horse with Dargle and Burke, under the plea of hedging.   Dargle was a friend of his, but he would be all the more vindictive on that account, if he suspected he had been wronged.   Burke, too, was a dangerous man to try and get the best of.   Well, thank goodness for the mist.

At any other time Tom Ring's honest face would have put him in better spirits.

"No horse will go down to the post so fit, Captain.   It will be like old times again, seeing you coming in first in the Warleigh stripes.   Look at him, he is the picture of what a chaser should be," said the trainer, as he came up to him in the paddock, looking as proud as he did on his wedding-day.

Amongst the knot of people gathered

round the favourite was Kate Cottingham, who was with her father and Jack Warleigh.

As Cecil came up, their eyes met, and in the look she seemed to tell him that he had her sympathies in what she knew was a trying time for him. He felt less uncomfortable after that, he would go through with it, and it would come off right. His qualms of conscience melted, and he only felt savage with his nephew, when he saw Jack and Kate together.

"Thank goodness," he said to himself, as the horses passed the post after the second race, "the worst part of the day is over." He was riding a horse of Lord Dargle's in the race before the Grand National—for some time he would be out of the way.

"Are you going to ride in this? think you might as well have left it alone," a voice whispered into his ear, and looking round he saw Colonel Beamish. "I should have thought that job of ours about enough for one day."

Cecil Warleigh did not answer him. It was a confounded piece of impertinence on Beamish's part, daring to talk to him like that.

He was riding to oblige Dargle, and he thought it might become very important for him to conciliate that high-spirited nobleman, who he knew was rather keen about picking up the race.

"Nick Holmes wanted Pat to ride in this race, but I told him to keep quiet for the National," said Kit Lukes to Beamish.

There was a horse trained in Holmes' stable entered for the hurdle race, which they had backed for a little money. If their horse got off well he would win, they believed, but he was an ill-tempered brute that often would not start. They were watching the race from the trainer's stand, which is almost opposite the starting post.

"Think Warleigh might have done the same, and I just told him so," answered Beamish.

"More fool you, he won't stand that sort of thing from you, if he is the man I take him to be," said the lawyer.

"We're out of it this time, I am afraid. That brute Wood-pecker is 'at his old games,'" he added, as the savage beast in which they were interested threw back his ears and refused to start.

"It won't much matter if we win on the National, but I'd like to win on this, just to show we're in luck. It doesn't look like it, though," said Beamish, as from the ring went up shouts of longer odds against Wood-pecker.

"He's off all right; no, by the Lord Harry; did ever man see such a brute? look at him;" and Kit Lukes gave vent to some red-hot language as Wood-pecker stopped dead, and lashed out at the horse that passed him.

"An' begorra, he's done a dale o' mischief this time," said a rich Irish brogue, just behind them, which belonged to Doctor Buckeen, late of the Lancers. "He got Cecil Warleigh that time, an' devil a bit of a race for the Grand National will Warleigh ride."

"Hang him, didn't I tell him he had better have stood down?" said Beamish, who had seen Wood-pecker lash out, and had heard Dr. Buckeen's exclamation.

"Keep quiet, you noisy idiot," snarled Kit Lukes, and Beamish felt the lawyer's hand clutch his arm convulsively. Lukes knew that the horse's heels had gone uncommonly near Cecil's boots, if they had not caught him. But as he watched the race, he continued. "No, look how he is riding—he's all right, and he'll win."

Kit Lukes was not troubled by the loss of the few pounds that he had on Wood-pecker. That no mishap should come to Cecil Warleigh was of far more importance to him than that he should win on the hurdle race. "It was a near shave, but it missed him," he remarked aloud.

"Bedad! I say, it just got 'um," repeated the Doctor.

Cecil seemed to be all right, however, he rode like the same great horseman he had always been, and no one could find fault with the way he won the race, which he did tolerably easily.

"Warleigh is in luck to-day," Kit Lukes heard some one say to Dr. Buckeen.

"But I'd like to have a look at that leg of his. Wood-pecker caught him, and if he is fit to ride in the Grand National, I'll eat him," replied the doctor.

CHAPTER XXV.

THE RACE FOR THE GRAND NATIONAL.

KIT LUKES hastened down from the Grand Stand, after the hurdle race was over, and got to the weighing room in time to see Cecil Warleigh weighed in.

Cecil looked rather paler than usual, and his teeth seemed to be clenched together as if he were in pain.

" Yes, won easy enough. Hope it is a good omen for the big race," he said to Dargle, after he had passed the scales, but his face grew whiter, and feeling in the pockets of his long great coat, which he had thrown over him, he pulled out a silver flask, and, putting it up to his lips, drained the contents.

" Didn't know you went in for that sort of thing before you rode a big race?" said Lord Dargle, looking at him rather hard.

Cecil didn't answer, but the colour came back into his face a little, and he looked less faint. Kit Lukes, however, saw that Dr. Buckeen was right—that brute, Wood-pecker, had caught him when he lashed out.

"He is a well plucked 'un though, and will stick to it, and see us through all right. Once let him get into the saddle and start, I don't care if he tumbles off in a faint, or pulls for us," Lukes said to himself, as he watched Cecil.

Cecil went into an inner room to change the jacket he wore for the red and black striped Warleigh colours. The lawyer noticed that he moved very tenderly, though he did his best not to limp, and he saw the mark on his breeches where he had been kicked. Blue Ruin was being saddled for the great race, but Nick Holmes and Pat Considine might look after that themselves. He wanted to be sure of Cecil.

The numbers were going up for the Grand National, and Lukes could hear the tumult of the ring. The Crier was being made a warmer favourite. Would it be too late to hedge? he asked himself, as he thought of Cecil's pale face. Suppose at that moment he had utterly collapsed.

"Thank heaven! he's all right so far," said Lukes—using a form of speech somewhat inappropriate, considering the work he was to be all right for—as Cecil came out of the dressing-room in the Warleigh colours.

Tom Ring, with his face wreathed in smiles, had come up to him.

"Well, Captain, if it was anyone else but you going to ride the Crier, I'd have been fit to die with envy—but you don't look well—does anything ail you?"

"No, I am all right, but I'll get on to the horse, and away from all this," answered Cecil, "get me the saddle, and I'll go and be weighed."

"That brute of Nick Holmes went near catching you, Captain Warleigh, when he lashed out at the start. I was in the trainer's stand and saw it," said Lukes, who was too anxious to keep quiet.

"Yes, but a miss is as good as a mile. I am ready for the Grand National, Mr. Lukes, thank you," answered Cecil, and as their eyes met, the lawyer saw that the other meant that it would be all right, though in his pain he was biting his lips till they bled.

The weighing-room was crowded.

"Hullo, Cecil! You don't look very well on it," said Bamborough, who was weighing to ride the Middy. "Hope you haven't been plunging too much on your mount, for I don't mind telling you now, that I am a good bit better than anyone knows. By George! I feel like a winner to-day, which you don't look."

"Hullo, mister! Whose colours are

those?" the professional jockey who was riding the Limpet was saying to Pat Considine.

"My own," answered Pat, who was sporting an orange and green jacket, which was more often seen at third-rate suburban meetings, and at out-of-the-way Continental affairs, than on any of the better known courses, "and may-be you'll remember 'em after to-day," he added.

"What are you going to do in the race, then? Jostle the favourite, or get in my way?" asked the jockey.

"No, win!" said Pat, who knew that he could afford the pleasure of boasting, for no human being who knew him could be influenced one way or the other by any word he might utter.

Jack Warleigh and a knot of his friends stood round the Crier, who looked big enough to carry Blue Ruin, who was being saddled a few yards off. Kit Lukes' nervous face grew calmer for a second or two, as he looked at the brave little mare that was going to land his great *coup* for him. "She's good enough to win on her merits," he thought for a moment, but for all that, he felt glad that her most dangerous opponent was to be made a dead 'un, and his restless eyes turned to Cecil Warleigh, who moving—

he could guess how painfully—was coming from the weighing-room.

"It's all right, but he's a well plucked 'un," Lukes said, and under his breath he muttered a sort of prayer. Suddenly his face changed, he hissed out a terrible oath. He could hear a Dublin brogue lifted up amongst the crowd round the Crier.

"It's that blathering ass, Buckeen," he said to Beamish, who was near him.

Dr. Buckeen had pushed through the crowd round the Crier and stood between Cecil and the horse.

"Cecil, me dear old boy! I say you're not fit to ride—don't tell me—I saw the Wood-pecker catch you, an' there's the mark on your breeches. You're worse hurt than you think, though if you're not suffering pain now, I'm a Dutchman!"

"You'd better mind your own business, and leave me alone, and be hanged to you, you officious ass!" answered Cecil, half mad with pain and annoyance, as he got into the saddle.

"But 'tis me own business, haven't I a pony on the horse? Sir John Warleigh, me Lord Dargle, I appale to ye. Don't let 'im ride," implored Buckeen; and without any more ceremony, he gripped Cecil's leg over the knee.

Cecil bit his cheek till it bled, but for all that he winced with pain.

"Captain Warleigh is the best judge as to whether he is fit to ride or not," said Jack, who considered the doctor's intrusion an impertinence. "I take it, he wouldn't wish to ride if he wasn't fit."

"But look here, Cecil—this fellow— Dr. What's-his-name is about right. There's something wrong with you—man alive! you're going to faint—here you— look and see what is wrong with him!" said Lord Dargle to the doctor: he was one of the proudest men in England, but had no nonsense about him, when his own interests were concerned.

"I'm all right, confound you—you d—d ignorant bogtrotter!" said Cecil, but his voice died away to a mumble, as a dull sense came over him that it was useless to struggle any longer. Then a clammy sweat broke out over his white face, and limp and faint, he slipped from the saddle into the arms of the doctor.

The doctor bared Cecil's leg over the knee, cutting away with a pocket-knife as if breeches-maker's bills were the merest trifles.

"And he was going to start to ride the Grand National steeple-chase, with a knee on 'im like that; faith, now it's free to do so, you can *see* it swelling!" exclaimed the doctor.

With professional pride, he stepped

back and pointed to the injured limb. He felt that he had gained a niche in the Temple of Fame, if only the Crier won, and that his name, together with that of Sir John Warleigh's, Cecil's, and the Crier, would go down to posterity in Sporting History.

"I am obliged to you, sir," said Jack Warleigh to the doctor, "but the question is, 'What can be done?' But there's not much doubt about that, though," he added, "Tom Ring will ride."

"Right, Sir John, and win," answered Tom Ring.

He was sorry for Cecil's disappointment, as he thought, at not riding the winner of the great race; still he could not help feeling a thrill of satisfaction, feeling sure that he was going to steer the Windmill Lodge crack to victory. When Cecil recovered from his faintness, he saw Tom Ring mounting the Crier, and he felt the Fates might do what they liked, he was out of it.

"He has put us 'in the cart,' confound him," said Beamish. "What can we do, Lukes? You know the market, can't we hedge?"

"Hedge! Not a tenth, not a twentieth of our money now. No, we've got to see it through, and trust to Pat Considine, Blue Ruin, and the chapter of accidents."

Then Cecil Warleigh remembered that he had one last chance. He thought of the hold he had over the trainer, and he called to mind the protestations the honest fellow had so often made, that he would do anything in the world to serve him, and show his gratitude.

"Tom," he said, laying his hand on the saddle, and whispering into his ear, "you must lose this race, or I'm clean broke, utterly smashed and disgraced. I was to have pulled. That's why I would ride."

Tom Ring had no time to answer, for Jack Warleigh came up, but he stared at Cecil, amazed, as if he thought the man he loved and looked up to, had suddenly gone mad; and his bewildered expression gradually changed to one of reproach and horror, as he took in the situation. He could not answer by word, and Cecil's eyes shifted away from him, as if he were unwilling to give him a chance of answering by gesture.

Jack led the horse to the gate of the paddock, and then went towards the stand; and Cecil, brushing past Dr. Buckeen, who was bothering him to have his leg bandaged up, at once limped after him, for he felt certain he was going to join Kate Cottingham and her father, who would be on one of the stands. And there she was, looking through her race-glasses at the horses doing their preliminary canter.

Cecil knew her face well enough to notice how anxious she was. He watched her, as Jack spoke a word or two to her, telling her, as he guessed, of the accident and the change of riders. For a second her pale face grew a shade or two paler, then, as she answered, the subtle charm of her eyes and voice, which he knew so well, seemed to be exercised with all its power on Jack.

" Oh, Captain Warleigh, how horribly unlucky ! " she said to Cecil, as he came forward ; " however, you will have to look on, and see some one else in your place."

Cecil did not answer, but he set his teeth, and vowed to himself that he would do his best to hate the woman who seemed to mock at him.

" After all, Cecil, it is not as if it were your first steeple-chase," said Jack, " you have won it before."

" Yes, one had one's past success to look back to. One knows how little there is in it all," answered Cecil, eyeing Kate meaningly.

" He is a grand horse," interrupted the General, as the Crier swept past the stand in his preliminary, and took the two hurdles, followed by little Blue Ruin.

" Hullo ! what's that ? that's a useful-looking mare," said the General, refer-

ring to his card. " Pat Considine's Blue
Ruin."

Cecil thought so too. Blue Ruin looked
a flyer, every inch of her ; after all, there
was no telling how good she might not be.

" No, the horse hasn't won yet," he
muttered.

" I never felt so interested, I never had
so much on," said Kate recklessly.

" Hope you haven't been plunging, Miss
Kate. I hate betting women ; particularly when I have to settle for them,"
said the General.

" Not more than I can pay myself,"
answered Kate.

Cecil watched the horses at the start,
and. gave a sigh of relief as they got
away at the first time of asking. Somehow it seemed to him that what was hap-
pening was a dream that he had dreamed
before, again and again.

The first horse to show in advance was
Jack Sheppard, Lord Bamborough on the
Middy was in the next lot of about half
a dozen, then came the two Irish horses,
the Frenchman, Paladine, the German,
Ulda, and the Epsom trained horse,
Limpet. Blue Ruin was in the last lot,
and Tom Ring on the Crier, lay right
back. . Cecil watched Tom Ring over the
first double, as if he hoped to read what
effect his last words had on him.

"No one down," said Kate.

They maintained much the same order over the next fence. Then the Middy and Master Dick headed Jack Sheppard, and the pair raced away and led by some half dozen lengths.

"Ulda is down; that puts one dangerous customer out of it," said the General, as the Hungarian horse came to grief at the third fence.

"By Jove, it's a strong field. That Middy is a rare good 'un, if Bamborough could ride him," said Cecil, as over the plough, past Valentine's Brook, the last-named horse came up to Master Dick.

The tail was beginning to lengthen, but still Tom Ring on the Crier lay back.

"The Crier is nowhere, he's not in the race," said Kate, with a glitter in her eyes and a shake in her voice as they came near the stand.

"Tom Ring is riding the race, as you did last year, Cecil," said the General.

Cecil did not answer. Was Tom going to wait a little too long? That is what he had meant to do.

At the next fence, two of the next lot came down. And at the water jump near the stand, Master Dick showed signs of how hot the pace had been, and Jack Sheppard took up the running, and led by some five lengths, followed by the

Middy, pulling hard, then came the Limpet, and some lengths off, Blue Ruin, and one of the Irishmen. Then the Crier, last of the still unbeaten horses. So they came to Becher's Brook, and over it into a long ploughed field, which Cecil thought would settle some of them.

"Look how well that thief, Pat Considine's going, Cecil. Hang it all, one doesn't want to see that lot win," said the General, as Blue Ruin came up very fast.

"But that lot will win!" cried Cecil, and there was a note of triumph in his voice, which he was too excited to conceal.

"No, look at Bamborough! By the Lord Harry, the Middy wins!" cried the General, as Lord Bamborough's horse passed Jack Sheppard, who had had enough of it, and whose mission, as a matter-of-fact, had only been to make the running for Blue Ruin, and led by a couple of lengths.

Lord Bamborough's many friends began to wish that they had been infected by that nobleman's confidence in his horse.

"The Middy walks in!" howled the ring, excitedly.

"No, he doesn't," said Cecil, whose knowledge of a race was instinctive. "Bamborough can't hold him."

Cecil was right, sure enough. The Middy had managed to get his bit fairly between his teeth, and was taking charge of his lordship !

At the end of the plough he had run himself out, and his rider was able to steady him a bit.

Jack Warleigh had hardly taken in the race, for he had been so engrossed in watching the Crier. Novice though he was, he felt sure there was plenty of go left in his great horse, and he bit his lips to restrain the anxiety he felt, and wondered why Tom Ring kept back so long. After getting over the plough, however, he began to come up to the others.

"It is all between those three," said Kate, as Blue Ruin, the Limpet, and the Middy took the first hurdle almost abreast.

"And one other," said Cecil, with a curse—which was heard and remembered by the others of the party—for now he saw that Tom Ring's affection for him was not strong enough to allow him to betray his master.

The Crier came up, and took the last hurdle into the run in, even with the Middy, who had galloped himself out, and some three lengths from Blue Ruin, who led.

"Blue Ruin wins, Blue Ruin wins !" howled the ring, who stood to win largely by Pat Considine's mount. But the plungers took heart. The Crier was now lying second, and the Limpet, who could stay for a week, was too slow to catch the leaders.

"By George! Blue Ruin is a good little mare," thought Cecil Warleigh, and he still hoped; though the Crier was at Blue Ruin's girths.

"Blue Ruin! The Crier! Blue Ruin wins! The Crier wins!" is alternately shouted from the stand.

"It's a dead heat!"

"Bosh! The Crier has won!" Cecil hears some one say.

Sick and faint, the pain in his knee suddenly seeming to master him, he had been unable to follow the finish, and again he had the feeling that he had seen it all before, some thousands of years ago.

"It's all right, my boy! The Crier, Blue Ruin, the Limpet," said the General, laying his hand on Cecil Warleigh's shoulder.

Then he sees something in Cecil's face that makes him look very grave. "Look here, you had better get away from here, you're looking very bad!" he added.

But it was not the look of faintness and pain in Cecil Warleigh's face that alarmed the General. There was a something else which told his secret to his old friend. Nevertheless, the General very tenderly looked after him, and saw him into a cab to be driven back to his hotel.

That evening, as they were travelling back to London, Kate Cottingham had some news to give her father. Jack Warleigh had asked her to marry him, and she had accepted.

"I'm glad of it," said the General, brightening up. He had been looking rather gloomy and old. "He is a good young fellow—won't set the Thames on fire, but he is honest, generous, and honourable, and a gentleman, and that's not what you can say of every one, nowadays. When we were young, we weren't any better than we should have been, but we used to stick to each other, and we had some notions of honour, but the lot who came after us don't seem to think that sort of thing carries any weight. I suppose they really know no better, poor beggars. However, that is not the point. Kate, my dear, you haven't had an over good bringing up; I would have been a better father to you if I had loved you less, and had had the pluck to send you away from me; you'll make Jack Warleigh a good wife, won't you, dear? He's a good youngster."

For the rest of the journey they were both very silent.

END OF VOL. I.

www.ingramcontent.com/pod-product-compliance
Lightning Source LLC
Chambersburg PA
CBHW020940120726
47905CB00008B/2601